Ash Child

Ash Child

A Gabriel Du Pré Mystery

PETER BOWEN

ST. MARTIN'S MINOTAUR
NEW YORK

www.minotaurbooks.com

Library of Congress Cataloging-in-Publication Data

Bowen, Peter.
    Ash child : a Montana mystery featuring Gabriel Du Pré / Peter Bowen.—1st. ed.
        p. cm.
    ISBN 0-312-28850-6
    1. Du Pré, Gabriel (Fictitious character)—Fiction. 2. Aged women—Crimes against—Fiction. 3. Sheriffs—Fiction. 4. Montana—Fiction. 5. Arson—Fiction. I. Title.

PS3552.O866 A93 2002
813'.54—dc21

                                                                                2001048745

First Edition: April 2002

10 9 8 7 6 5 4 3 2 1

For Barbara Peters

Ash Child

CHAPTER 1

Du Pré was pissed off. He was in a hospital and he didn't like hospitals.

He looked at the bottle on the rolling rack and then at the tubes that dripped the antibiotics into veins in his left arm.

He glared at the peaks his toes made in the blue sheets. He pushed the covers back and swung his legs over the side of the bed. He stood up, put his left hand on the rolling rack, and walked out of his room and down the hall.

"Good morning," said the nurse at the station. She was busily filling out forms.

"Good morning," said Du Pré. "Can I maybe get my clothes, leave now?"

The nurse didn't look up from her records.

"Du Pré," she said, "quit whining."

"Yah," said Du Pré.

"It was the flat hands-down worst appendix seen here in a

1

long, long time. You waited till it busted. Time the surgeon got in there, it was a mess. If you'd come in when it began to hurt, you'd've been home. Several days ago."

"Umph," said Du Pré.

"You cowboys," said the nurse, shutting one folder and opening another, "have the smarts of anvils. Make a good cowboy, you catch a sheep-herder and kick his brains out."

"Yah," said Du Pré.

"So why don't you go down to the kitchen and ask Isabel to make you some hot milk. It will help you sleep."

Hot milk, Du Pré thought. Jesus. Hot milk.

The nurse looked up.

"Look," she said, "you'll probably be able to go home the day after tomorrow. They won't be able to close up the wound until the infection is gone. You'll have to pack it, or have someone pack it for you. But the doctor'll let you go Thursday."

"Uh," said Du Pré.

A door banged. Boot heels sounded on the polished linoleum.

"Visitin' hours! Visitin' hours, you snipe-nosed pup! I came to see muh illegitimate son. Gab-reel Doo Pray. I am his dear ol' daddy, though it pains me to admit it. Now, outta my way 'fore I stuff that flashlight up yer ass."

The nurse looked at Du Pré.

"You have a visitor," she said. "Please go and see him. Tell Ron to come and see me."

Du Pré started to push the rolling rack toward the door.

"Don't forget the hot milk!" said the nurse, not looking up.

Du Pré pulled open the door.

Booger Tom was standing there, with his bony old finger in the chest of a young security guard who was backed against the wall.

"Old man," said Du Pré, "it is good to see you!"

"It's past visiting hours," said the kid, looking terrified.

"I'm gonna kill him," snarled Booger Tom, "I am. Goddamn government innerference ever' whar a man turns. Can't even go and see his bastard son!"

2

"Ron," said Du Pré, "the nurse, she want talk to you."

"I'll scalp yah!" said Booger Tom to the kid, who was moving very rapidly past Du Pré.

Du Pre' turned and led Booger Tom down the hall to his room. He went in and sat on the bed and pointed at the flowered-print chair.

"Jesus," said Booger Tom, "folks die in these damn places, ya know. Let's go."

"No," said Du Pré.

"All right," said Booger Tom. He lifted the huge book he was carrying. HOLY BIBLE.

It gurgled.

Booger Tom flipped up a port on the spine and pulled out a little spigot, and he went to the sink and filled half a plastic glass with whiskey. He ran cold water in the glass. He handed it to Du Pré.

Du Pré swallowed it.

He handed the glass back.

Booger Tom mixed another. Another.

Du Pré finally sighed and sat back on the bed and pulled the rolling rack over so the needles in his arm wouldn't pull.

"These places ain't civilized," said Booger Tom. "They's deddy-cated to healin' the sick, and you'd think they'd be civilized about it."

Du Pré laughed.

"And I 'spect ya can't smoke, neither," said Booger Tom, "and screwin' is outta the question."

Du Pré laughed.

"No wonder folks die on the street," said Booger Tom. "Easy to see why they'd want to, been in a place like this."

"Yah," said Du Pré.

"So when's they lettin' you out?" said Booger Tom. He had a sack of Bull Durham in his hand. He fiddled out a paper with his fingers and rolled a smoke, one-handed. He licked the paper and put the cigarette in his mouth.

"Way I see it," he said, "I gave ya one a these they'd throw us both out of here."

Du Pré opened the drawer of the nightstand and took out a tin of snoose. He took a pinch and put it behind his lower lip.

Booger Tom scratched a kitchen match on the seat of his canvas pants and the flame flared and he touched the end of the cigarette with it.

A couple of quarts of water flew in the door and soused Booger Tom.

He sat there for a moment, blinking, while water ran off his face and his hat.

The cigarette was a sodden mess.

Booger Tom looked at the door.

"I don't care if you want to read the Bible," said the nurse. "Read the Bible all night. Pray quietly. But you cannot smoke in here, you old son of a bitch, and if you want to be wearing your ass for a hat just try that again."

"Yes, ma'am," said Booger Tom.

"Praise Jesus!" said the nurse. Her shoes squeaked a little on the waxed floor as she went back to her station.

Du Pré looked at his friend.

"You are wet," he said. "There are towels in the bathroom."

"That's all right," said Booger Tom, "I been wetter'n this a lot. She is dead set against tobacco, and she has made her point."

Booger Tom held up the Bible and Du Pré nodded.

He made Du Pré another drink. Du Pré gave him the tin of snoose.

"I ain't seen tin ones of these in thirty year," said Booger Tom. "Where'd you find it?"

Du Pré smiled.

"Catfoot chewed it," he said. "Me, I found couple hundred of these, the tool shed."

Booger Tom nodded.

"Madelaine here?" he said.

"Visiting hours," said Du Pré. "She got sick aunt, Billings, she is there, too."

Booger Tom nodded.

"Everybody sends their best," said the old man.

Du Pré looked at the Bible.

"Bart done give me that," said Booger Tom. "Said he had it made long time ago and forgot to throw it out."

Du Pré laughed.

Bart Fascelli, drunk for years, bad drunk, been dry a long time now. But he was a good friend.

"I sorta thought you'd be about ready to get the hell out of here," said Booger Tom, "so I just got in the truck and come down. When are they springin' you?"

"Thursday," said Du Pré.

"A bad appendix," said Booger Tom. "I still got mine."

"Good," said Du Pré.

Booger Tom chewed thoughtfully.

He looked at the ceiling.

"Somebody done killed Maddy Collins," he said.

Du Pré sat up.

Maddy Collins was a nice addled old lady who lived a mile or so outside Toussaint. She had been in her little red house as long as Du Pré could remember. She didn't come to church or to town much. She worked in her flower beds. Beautiful flowers. She had a good water right and she'd kept it.

"Benny looked it over, called the State Police come look, they couldn't find nothin'."

Du Pré shook his head.

"Killed her in her house," said Booger Tom. "Beat her head in with a hatchet."

"Jesus," said Du Pré.

"Old Maddy Collins," said Booger Tom. "I done knowed her when she was a damn pretty woman."

Du Pré nodded.

"Enough," said the nurse from the doorway.

Booger Tom got up. He had put the big Bible in the closet, on the bottom.

"See you soon," he said.

The nurse smiled at Du Pré.

Booger Tom walked out and she switched off the light.

CHAPTER
2

Benny lifted up the yellow plastic tape that ran from stake to stake around Maddy Collins's little yellow house.

I remembered it as red, Du Pré thought. He went over to the wall and looked at it. The yellow paint was a few years old. He took out his pocketknife and scraped.

It was white underneath.

Du Pré shook his head.

"What?" said Benny.

Du Pré laughed.

"I think this house is red and it is not," he said.

"Been yellow long's I been here," said Benny. "What color is it underneath?"

"White," said Du Pré.

Benny shrugged. He unlocked the padlock on the front door and they went in. The house was musty and stank of old blood.

Benny switched on the lights. Two floor lamps with brass bases and red glass shades came on.

"She was right there," he said.

The coroner had outlined Maddy's body in chalk powder. She had been sprawled out, like a child making snow angels.

"Hit her once," said Benny, "hatchet went right through her left eye and into her brain four inches or so. She died then, coroner said."

Du Pré nodded.

"Just the one blow so there weren't no spray," said Benny. "She bled a lot there." He pointed at a dark thick stain on the worn Persian carpet.

"Hadn't been raped. Some of these bastards like rapin' old ladies, I guess. Hadn't been touched. Guy turned around and walked out and left the door open, or we'd a not likely found her for months. She didn't have much to do with anybody."

Du Pré nodded.

No, she didn't. Some mean kids tried to soap her windows one Halloween and she filled their butts with rock salt.

Du Pré looked behind the front door.

An old double-barreled shotgun stood against the wall. Maddy had put two little nails there to hold the barrels, so the shotgun wouldn't be knocked over. He picked it up and broke it open.

Two brass bases in the chambers. Du Pré broke the gun further and the shells were pushed up and he lifted them out.

Reloaded.

Du Pré shook them.

Too light for lead.

Rock salt.

"She peppered them kids ten years ago," said Benny. "They'd be in their twenties now. Far as we could tell, none of 'em held it against her. Ain't a one of 'em livin' here now. Girls are married and one the boys is in the Marines and the other's workin' construction in Seattle."

Du Pré nodded.

"State cops they find nothing?"

Benny shook his head.

"Vacuumed the carpet and got cat hairs and her hairs and that old dog she had died two years ago," said Benny. "Maddy liked her flowers but hated housework I guess."

Du Pré nodded.

The house smelled old. Old woman, old clothes, old breath, old shoes.

"Two fellers come and did the work here," said Benny. "They was here most a two days, left, said they didn't find dick. Report came back so I call over there, talk to some lieutenant, Probst or somethin' like that. He said they have three or four of these a year in Montana, no evidence, no motive, like somebody just stopped here a moment and killed somebody and went on. Don't steal nothin', don't stay long enough to shed hairs, don't touch anything."

Du Pré nodded.

He went past the outline and looked into the bedroom.

An old four-poster with a velvet canopy and spread and pillows with a lot of needlepoint on them. Marble-topped dresser and nightstand.

Nice things, old things.

Du Pré tried to remember if she had family.

"Husband died in fifty-six," said Benny. "Maddy was damn near ninety. Eighty-eight. Good shape, you know she worked in them gardens all of the time."

She had been small and wiry. A little dried-apple face. A faded old sunbonnet.

"They didn't have any kids and we're still looking for relatives. She didn't leave a will. Lived on Social Security. Place was paid for and she raised vegetables. A lot of canned stuff in the pantry and the cellar."

Du Pré nodded.

"There was about eight hundred dollars in the top dresser drawer," said Benny, "but not a single letter or a card or anything like that. Seems like she didn't have any kin at all."

Du Pré looked through the bedroom window. There was a woodstove out in the back, under a little arbor, and some lilac bushes. A few Siberian elms. A couple of paper birches down by the little ditch. She drew her water from Sipple's Creek; the headgate was a half-mile up the larger ditch that ran on to Loughey's place.

"Lieutenant said he doubted we'd ever find the killer 'less it was some kid who gets beered up and brags about it," said Benny.

Du Pré nodded.

He stood up and he felt the wound in his belly pull a little. The damn thing was draining and he had to pack it with fresh dressings twice a day.

Dakin's solution. Some yellowish stuff, soak the gauze and pack it in the wound. Pull it out. But the lips of the wound wanted to heal and if the gauze wasn't just right they stuck together.

A week, the doctor said, we can close you up.

Du Pré sighed.

"I will go have a smoke," he said. He walked back through the living room and past the outline of Maddy on the carpet and he went through the door and around the house.

He looked at the lilacs.

They were very dry. The weather had been hot and dry for weeks. The air was thick and hazy. Forest fires were burning to the west, hundreds of thousands of acres of timber.

The Wolf Mountains had had one little fire, but it was lightning that had caused it and it was put out quickly.

Du Pré's nose prickled. In Missoula, far to the west, the schools were closed and many people couldn't go outside.

The grass crackled under Du Pré's boots.

Dry.

Me, I have never seen it this dry.

The grass catches fire all we do, run.

Raymond, Du Pré's son-in-law, had put a sprinkler on the roof of their house, and it ran constantly. If fire came close, it would come so fast there would be no time to douse anything.

Benny opened the back door of the house.

"God damn, it's dry," he said. "The mountains are there, I guess, they must be them shadows."

Du Pré laughed.

Benny was well educated, but he had wanted to be Sheriff and so he tried to talk like local people, who spoke a dialect. He couldn't get it right.

Benny and Susan, been here twenty years or so, Du Pré thought, Susan buys the Toussaint Saloon, she is tired of school-teaching. Benny taught too.

Them shadows.

Me, I say, shadows, them. Metchif.

"Du Pré?" said Benny. "This is a god damned shame, you know. She was a crazy old lady never bothered anybody and somebody just killed her for no reason. She didn't have friends, let alone enemies. She didn't speak to anybody much, never said anything in the grocery store or the saloon. She did come in, have a red beer every once in a while."

Du Pré nodded.

Mornings, red beer time. Beer and tomato juice.

Toussaint's old people did that. Red beer in the morning.

Maybe she talked to somebody at the saloon.

Du Pré had never seen her there, but he didn't go there in the mornings.

"I asked at the bar," said Benny, "the old folks there. Maddy would come in and have her red beer. But she always sat down at the end of the bar, humming a little. Never said boo to anyone."

Du Pré nodded.

He looked to the west.

The sky was white and hazy, and the sun yellow and vague.

CHAPTER

3

Bart finished the little ditch. He turned the slit bucket up against the arm of the backhoe and shut off the diesel engine. He got down from the seat and went to the ditch and looked critically at his work.

"Fair," he said, "just fair."

Du Pré went to the new headgate and pulled it up and water flooded the new channel, turning the broken earth to a slurry of yellow-brown mud.

The little ditch ran along the crest of a shallow ridge. When the water got to the end of the ditch the level rose and it began to flow over the downhill edge. For two hundred yards a spreading stain of water moved through clumps of yellow grass.

"New haymeadow," said Du Pré. The soil was good here, and in a year there would be lush hay thick in the field.

Bart picked up a stick of sagebrush and flexed it. It broke with a *snap!*

"God, it's dry," he said.

Seventy-one days without rain.

Little puffy clouds hung above the Wolf Mountains. Dew, fallen at night, evaporated by the sun, turning to thick cottony clouds. In the night, it would be dew again. But each day the clouds were smaller.

"All closed off now," said Bart, looking at the mountains. For the first time in anyone's memory, the Forest Service had closed the mountains. Fire danger. A ranger had come to listen to any complaints. He had said conditions were worse than they had been in 1910.

Nineteen ten.

A dry year like this year. And then there had been a dry lightning storm, and small fires started.

Two days later high winds, winds of ninety and a hundred miles an hour, came without warning. In half an hour the small fires were giants and eating whole square miles of forest in minutes. Firestorms blew up, columns of flame that threw burning debris miles downwind, and more fires began and soon grew.

Western Montana burned.

It was dry in 1911, too.

Montana burned again, east of the Great Divide.

The forests came back. Lodgepole pine. It was ninety-odd years later and time for all the lodgepole pine to burn again.

Du Pré wondered how long it would be before the Wolf Mountains would light the sky bloodred.

It would happen.

Soon.

"Not a damn thing to do," said Bart.

Du Pré shook his head.

People here were used to grass fires. The ranchers made sure that they had wide swaths around their houses and buildings that had little or no fuel in them. They all had water tanks for their trucks, and hoses run around their compounds.

The forests were another matter.

The Wolf Mountains were steep and dangerous, a bad place to fight a fire and a worse place to try to run from one.

"Hunting seasons are closed, at least," said Bart.

Every year hordes of hunters came here, to go to the public lands in the Wolf Mountains, and every year some asked to hunt on the private lands on the plains below.

The answer from the ranchers was always no.

Some hunters—the out-of-state ones were the worst—didn't bother to ask, and seemed to think that buying a hunting license also bought a ticket to all Montana.

Post fences near ranch gates had boots on the tops of them. The boots had once been on hunters who, caught trespassing, were told to take them off and leave them and walk out.

Over the rocks and cactus in their stockinged feet.

"We got all of the cattle down from the high country," said Bart. "So did the Martins. Few others left their stock up there. That's a big gamble."

Du Pré nodded.

If the mountains burned, the cattle would probably die.

If the mountains burned.

The mountains were going to burn.

They always had.

The Blackfeet had gotten their name from their soot-stained leggings and moccasins, for they set fires constantly to run game. Sometimes the fires were catastrophic. In 1826 the Blackfeet had set fires in a dry time like this and seven villages had been caught by walls of flame and hundreds of people killed.

The next year it was wet, and the grass was so abundant the Plains tribes called it the Year of Fat Buffalo.

"When I was a kid," said Bart, "in Chicago, I remember one August day. It was cloudy and terribly still and I had asthma and I could hardly breathe. I was scared and I didn't know why. And then the sky got black in the southwest and a terrible storm came in and there were bad tornadoes all around and this has the same feel that day did."

Du Pré nodded.

I am scared of this some, he thought. Scared of the fires, scared they start and we can't stop them.

Du Pre remembered the name the Blackfeet had given to the year before the Year of Fat Buffalo. That was the Year of Roasted Blackfeet. The men who had set the fires were killed.

Long time gone.

"I got to go plow a firebreak around the main Martin house," said Bart. "Morgan Martin hates to give up her shrubbery. She said she hated the thought of that logpile she lives in going up in flames more."

Du Pré nodded.

The Martin ranch's main house was over a hundred years old. It had been built of logs, and designed by some famous architect who had designed huge log mansions in the Adirondacks.

The Martins' money was very old and they had very old beautiful things.

"She sent the paintings away already," said Bart. "You know, every one of them has its own aluminum case, airtight, and a nitrogen bottle that fills the case? I suppose all those Impressionist paintings are worth it. She said she has three Van Goghs that are actual Van Goghs."

Du Pré thought of the Dutch painter and his sad life.

Cut off his ear, shoot himself.

Him paint, he use stove wood and matchsticks for brushes.

Van Gogh.

Sometimes this country look like what Van Gogh sees.

Bart ran the tractor up on the trailer and he went to the dump truck he pulled it with and got in and started the big diesel engine.

He opened the cab door.

"Who would kill old Maddy Collins?" he said. Bart looked hurt.

Du Pré walked over to the truck. "Don't know."

"She was just an eccentric old woman," said Bart. "She just lived her life alone and didn't bother anyone."

Du Pré nodded.

"You and Benny have no ideas?" said Bart. "If you need help, I would get it for you."

Bart, with his millions of dollars. Always ready to write a check. Hire some detectives.

Piss everybody off.

"Maybe we think of something," said Du Pré, "need some things done, a laboratory."

"Call Foote if you do," said Bart. "I'll talk to him."

Charles Foote, the lawyer who took care of Bart's money, and Bart, too. Elegant, tough, smart, that Foote.

"Don't think of anything," said Du Pré.

Bart got down from the cab and looked at Du Pré.

"It just doesn't make any sense," he said. "Nothing was taken, there was no robbery. She wasn't raped. She didn't have any enemies. She didn't speak to anyone."

Du Pré nodded.

Bart was very upset.

The murder was senseless.

People like to make sense of things, even if there is none.

"It has to be someone from around here," said Bart.

Du Pré shrugged.

Maybe.

"No reason at all," said Bart softly.

"*Non, non,*" said Du Pré, "there is a reason. I just don't see it yet, me."

Bart looked at Du Pré.

"There is always a reason, Bart," said Du Pré.

CHAPTER

4

Madelaine was in the bar, slicing limes and lemons. She looked up when Du Pré came in.

He sat and she made him a whiskey ditch. She put it in front of him and went back to the limes.

"You have your drink," she said, "you go to my house you turn on the water."

Du Pré nodded.

Shit. I know. There is not so much water coming out of the tap. Water table it is dropping.

Jacqueline, Raymond, they got a real deep well, Catfoot put that one in. He say, I am drilling this well I go down more, some-day I don't have to go down more.

But Madelaine's well is not so deep.

Shit.

"I try to get the well digger," said Madelaine, "they got a tape machine, the telephone, say, leave a number for us we call you next year maybe."

Shit.

Catfoot's old well rig it is out back there, Raymond and my daughter Jacqueline, old bastard of a truck it has not been running for maybe twenty years. Du Pré tried to remember when the old Chevrolet had last been started. It was on blocks, and the tires were in the toolshed with some others, all on rims.

Tires all flat, probably.

Engine rusted shut.

Madelaine's well is going dry.

I hate working engines.

"You hate working engines," said Madelaine. "I know that but you don't fix my well there my garden it is dead. Flowers, too."

Du Pré nodded.

Me, I know what I do, next few days.

He finished his ditch and went out and got in the cruiser and he drove to the little place where he had been raised and where his daughter and her husband and their twelve kids lived now.

Du Pré pulled off the road near the white lilac bushes that Catfoot had planted. He shut the engine off and waited.

A mob of kids came pelting round the shrubs, laughing.

"Grandpère!" said Berne.

"Yes!" said Alcide.

"Yes," said Du Pré. He got out and he hugged a lot.

"You come!" said Alcide, taking Du Pré by the hand.

He led him around the house and across the yard to the long toolshed where Catfoot's welding equipment and machine tools were.

The old well-drilling rig was sitting by the open sliding doors. The tires were on it. The hood was up and Raymond and several small boys were in the engine compartment.

"Give me the three-eighths," said Raymond. "Don't drop it this time."

A small, grubby hand held out the socket.

Raymond put the socket on the driver and reached down for the bolt.

He strained.

The socket slipped off the old bolt and Raymond cursed long and very fluently.

"Jacqueline cut your nuts off your sons say those words," said Du Pré. He looked in the engine compartment.

"They got to learn all them words," said Raymond. "Man needs them words sometimes."

"SON OF A COCKSUCKING PISSPOT SHITHEAP!" said four small voices.

Raymond pulled back from the engine and he looked at his sons.

"That is pret' good," he said, "pret' damn good. Now, you don't got to practice, your mother."

"Yes, Papa," they said.

"You say that," said Raymond, holding up his hand, a finger leaking blood, "you say that, you cut your finger, old goddamn engine."

"Yes, Papa," said the boys.

"You don't say it other times," said Raymond.

"No, Papa," said the boys.

"It is important," said Raymond.

The boys said nothing and looked as solemn as four little owls.

"Your mother don't like them words," said Raymond, "specially you use them, your sisters."

"They already know them," said Hercule.

Raymond sighed.

"So," he said, looking at Du Pré, "I think this old piece of shit run now maybe."

Du Pré nodded.

Raymond put the air cleaner back on top of the carburetor and he stepped back off the bumper.

"You try it maybe?" he said.

Du Pré went around to the driver's door and got in. The old

cab looked very familiar. He had ridden in it a lot. For years it had been Catfoot's welding rig, and then he got another truck and put an old well drill on the back of the Chevy.

The drill was oiled and the hydraulic hoses were new.

"OK," said Raymond.

Du Pré turned the key and pressed the big silver starter button on the dash.

RRRRRRRRRRRRrrrrrrrrrrrrrrrr.

"Stop," said Raymond. He took a can of ether and sprayed it into the carburetor.

RRRRRRRRRrrrrrrrrrrrrBANGBANGbangrumble.

The old engine settled down and purred along.

"Somebody pour oil, the engine," said Raymond, "it is in good shape. Me, I think maybe I make some money now, wells."

"Yah," said Du Pré. He is a good son-in-law, good Métis man, does what he can, feed his family.

"Madelaine's well it is going dry," said Du Pré.

"We do it first," said Raymond, "see if I fix this drill right. It is pret' bad rusted."

Du Pré went back to the control box and fiddled a minute and then the auger began to turn. He pushed the lever back and the auger stopped.

"Good," he said.

Raymond got in the truck and the gearbox bucked and ground for a moment. He double-clutched and the old transmission locked into reverse and the truck lurched deliberately back.

Raymond stuck his thumb up.

"I go to Madelaine's," he said. "Where is the well?"

"North side," said Du Pré. "I go there, guide you in."

Du Pré drove to Madelaine's and parked out on the street.

Raymond backed the old truck in. Du Pré stopped him. He found a long piece of wood to push the electrical cable up with. He held it three feet higher while Raymond backed the truck beneath it.

Du Pré let the cable down. His shoulder twinged from the work.

Old, I am getting old. Things hurt didn't used to.

Raymond went back and back and Du Pré signaled him to stop.

They walked back to the little wellcap and Du Pré bent and lifted it. A submersible pump at the bottom of a steel pipe.

"Well," said Raymond, "there is even some six-inch, behind the toolshed. I maybe pull this while you maybe weld up two of them eight-foots?"

"Sixteen feet, a lot," said Du Pré.

Raymond shrugged.

"We are doing this we do it maybe, don't have to do it again. I see this program, the TV, say maybe we are having a dry time, haven't had one like this, thousand years. So maybe we give Madelaine eight feet more."

"It is good sand down there," said Du Pré, "should be."

He left Raymond fiddling with the wellhead cap.

Du Pré found the torches and tanks and he wheeled them out in front of the toolshed.

He found two eight-foot sections of pipe.

He set them up on the chickenfoot stands Catfoot had made from rebar and scraps.

He put on the welder's coat and the mask and he lit the torch and began to lay bead around the joint.

Fire stabbed from the torch and drops of hot metal fell on the ground.

CHAPTER 5

"They stitch you up, Du Pré?" said Madelaine, when Du Pré came out of the doctor's office.

"Couple little pieces tape," said Du Pré, "that is all. They say, that tape falls off, you will be all stuck together."

They walked out to the old cruiser and got in and Du Pré headed for home.

The doctor in Cooper was there two days a week, so they only had thirty-five miles to drive.

Du Pré pulled into the lot beside the Toussaint Saloon twenty-two minutes later.

"Well," said Madelaine, "maybe we go in there, I have some pink wine and you have ditch or two and we talk, Maddy Collins."

Du Pré nodded.

People had talked about Maddy for a few days, and they thought of her, but there was so little to say.

No one had known her. She didn't talk to anyone. No one ever visited her. She lived alone. Not exactly a hermit, not exactly a citizen of Toussaint.

They went in, and Susan Klein smiled at them. She was looking at the television.

"Funniest program ever on television," she said, "C-Span. Those fat bastards in Congress'd do better they heard that satire is supposed to be intentional."

She brought them drinks.

"Maddy," she said.

Du Pré nodded.

Madelaine looked at him.

"She was scared, scared bad of something," said Madelaine. "Walked with her head down, all time, mumbling."

Du Pré looked at her.

Madelaine looked at Susan.

"She that way all the time?" she said. "Is it just me sees her like that."

"All the years I knew her," said Susan, "she wasn't all there I don't think. She would come in here three or four days a week and I would give her a red beer. I took her dollar and gave her her quarter and that was that. But some of the other old folks would come then, too, and she'd sit down there, the end of the bar, and she'd stare at the bottles there and she'd sip her beer and off she'd go."

Du Pré held up his hands.

"She talk maybe to Van Den Heuvel?" he said. The big clumsy Belgian Jesuit tended the flock of Catholics in Cooper County, who tended him. Since he had arrived, he had knocked himself unconscious seven times, shutting his head in his car door.

"Was she Catholic?" said Susan.

"She is Irish maybe," said Du Pré. "I go and see him."

"I," said Susan Klein, "will go and call him." She went off to the telephone near the kitchen.

"Where she is," said Madelaine, "it is easy for someone, come in through the pasture, park on the highway. They don't know when she is killed?"

Du Pré shook his head.

"Benny don't say," he said. "I don't see the report yet, the state police either. Maybe they don't send it yet."

"No mail either," said Madelaine.

Du Pré shook his head.

"She have a telephone?" said Madelaine.

Du Pré nodded. Old black one with the dial that spins.

"I see her sometimes," said Madelaine, "I wave but she never wave back, never look up, she is walking along, looking at the ground, talking to herself."

Du Pré nodded.

"Me, I should have done something," said Madelaine. "Go by her house take her some bread."

Du Pré smiled. My Madelaine, heal all the world she can.

"She don't want nobody," said Du Pré. "We leave her alone she wants that."

You could be crazy here and no one would bother you, unless you were the sort of crazy who was dangerous.

Susan Klein came back. She shook her head.

"Father Van Den Heuvel," she said, "didn't know who Maddy was. You know how bad his eyes are."

The priest wore glasses so thick his eyes swam behind them, huge and pale blue.

"So there is nothing," said Madelaine.

"No," said Du Pré, "it is just what is there we cannot see."

"OK," said Madelaine, "so you go and see that Benetsee, he is the one sees things no one else can."

"You come?" said Du Pré.

Madelaine shook her head.

"It is Friday, remember," she said. "Prime rib tonight, Susan got a lot of work, we got to start now."

Du Pré smiled and he got off his stool and he turned to go to the door.

"Du Pré!" said Susan Klein. She held up a jug of the awful screw-top wine the old man liked. And some sacks of Bull Durham.

Wine and tobacco, I bring the old goat, his apprentice here for meat later.

Wine, tobacco, meat.

Du Pré took the things from Susan and went out and put them on the front seat of the cruiser.

He was wearing a shirt with the sleeves cut off at the shoulder and boots and jeans. He was hot.

Cowboys don't wear shorts, and they don't wear short-sleeved shirts, Du Pré thought.

I don't know why.

He got in and started the engine and he drove up the bench road and along it, dust billowing out east behind him. There was a strong breeze from the west.

Fire start it feed on this good, Du Pré thought. His skin felt tight.

He could smell the burning forests three hundred and more miles to the west.

Fire in the mountains, make its own weather, clouds, more lightning.

It will all burn someday.

The tall grass around Benetsee's cabin was yellow and dead. The roots were still alive.

That grass, it waits. Waits for water, then it grows. Wait a long time it has to.

Du Pré didn't pull off in the grass to park the way he usually did. It was so bad now the hot muffler on his car could start a fire, and once a fire began it would be very hard to put out.

The wind was freshening. More of it. Sometimes, mid-August, there were winds a hundred miles an hour. Fires start they move a hundred miles an hour, too.

Du Pré looked off to the west. The sky was all white with dust and smoke.

He took the wine and tobacco out of the car and he went around the back of the house and down the path that went to the flood meadow where Benetsee had his sweat lodge.

The lodge was open and the firepit was cold and the wood and stones lay beside it. No fresh rick, ready to touch off.

The little creek ran as high as usual, though; it was fed by deep springs up at the foot of the mountains.

The deep pool that you plunged into when you came out of the sweat was clear and cold. Little brook trout darted out from the weeds to grab something and then they ducked back in.

A kingfisher flew past, a blur of bright blue and black.

GAAAAAACCCKKKK! it screamed, and then it landed on the limb of a cottonwood and looked down at the water.

"Old man," said Du Pré, "I need help. There is an old woman killed no one knows anything. She was very lonely and I need your help."

Du Pré set the wine and tobacco down on a stump by the creek. He walked back up the hill and got in his cruiser, started the engine, and backed out to the road.

Nothing to see.

I got to go back to that house, maybe I sleep there, outside, where I can hear.

Du Pré sighed.

It was even hot at night, never getting colder than seventy degrees.

He tried to remember if that had ever happened before.

No.

It always got down to forty degrees or so.

It always had, every night.

CHAPTER 6

Du Pré walked around Maddy Collins's little yellow house. The paint was old but had been well applied and care had been taken. The trim was peeling. Some people would have painted it two years ago, some would wait another three.

The flower beds were meticulously tended, but the hot weather had shriveled them and even a few days without water had killed many of the fragile plants. There were tiny little weeds, grasses that had found water and sprouted, but they were only days old.

How long was she dead before she was found?

Why was she found?

The front door was left open?

Who found her?

Who, for Chrissakes, killed this odd old woman?

Benetsee, damn you, you are gone I need you. It is just me and I do not know where to begin.

Benny doesn't know. Benny, he is a good Sheriff, but this is too much for him, he hates it.

Me, I am good at finding things out.

The clouds over the Wolf Mountains were bigger than they had been in the morning. More water had evaporated and risen and condensed.

Maybe some lightning in them.

Du Pré went to a shed and opened the door and looked in. It had a bench and piles of flowerpots and sacks of fertilizer and sphagnum moss and wood chips.

Du Pré shut the door.

There was an old car, an Oldsmobile, parked next to the house, and the garage door was down. The garage was separate from the house, and small, put up probably back in the 1920s when automobiles were narrow and much like buggies.

Du Pré slid the bolt and lifted the door.

Piles of boxes and bags of things were stacked front to back in the garage. Du Pré opened one of the black plastic bags.

Old newspapers.

She hoarded worthless things.

Du Pré slid the door back down and shot the bolt home. He looked in the car and tried the door. It was locked. The car was spotless inside, very well cared for.

Probably had twenty thousand miles put on it in forty years. Du Pré guessed it was made in the late 1950s.

He went back to the front of the house. The padlock was shut and the tape up.

Get the key from Benny.

Du Pré drove over to Cooper, west of Toussaint, on Cooper's Creek, the largest stream that came from the Wolf Mountains. Once Cooper had been a stop for freighters with the long Democrat freight wagons and ox teams, and then the town had hoped for the railroad, but that had not come. It had gone on the north side of the mountains.

Cooper was like a lot of little Montana towns, dying slowly, not enough trade to support businesses as people were forced off their lands by costs that rose and beef that didn't.

Du Pré drove through the little downtown, more buildings boarded up than weren't. He pulled in in front of the little Sheriff's office. It had three cells in the back and two offices in front. It had been built as cheaply as possible, of cinder block and concrete. The cells were old. They had been taken out of the basement of the county building. The county building was closed, unsafe, and court was held in another small cinder block building.

I am a kid, Du Pré thought, there are five hundred, maybe more people here, now there are half that maybe.

But they did have a new school, a high school, with lots of shiny computers and a gymnasium.

Du Pré went into the office. The dispatcher was there but no one else. Du Pré didn't like her, and she didn't like him.

"Benny?" said Du Pré.

"Back in a minute," said the woman. She went back to the magazine on her desk.

Du Pré went outside and rolled a smoke. He lit it and looked to the west.

Hazy, some clouds far off, no rain coming.

Benny came around the corner of the grocery store, eating a horrid doughnut.

He waved to Du Pré.

Du Pré waited for him, smoking.

"You want to look at the report?" said Benny. "Got mine and got the state one this morning."

"Who find her?" said Du Pré.

"I did," said Benny softly. "Margie is the mail carrier, she saw that Maddy's door was open, and still open the next day so she turned right around and came in to tell me and I went right out."

Du Pré nodded.

Left the door open. Wanted her to be found, maybe.

Or he just forgot.

Du Pré sighed.

He followed Benny inside and Benny got the reports and Du Pré put them under his arm and walked out and up the street to the tavern.

The woman behind the bar looked up when he came in and she mixed a ditch for him. Du Pré put two dollars on the bar and took the drink to a table by the window. He fished his reading glasses out of his shirt pocket and put them on.

"Old age is hell," said the woman behind the bar. She grinned.

Du Pré grunted.

He looked at Benny's report first.

Benny had been told by the mail lady, and he had driven right out. He found Maddy lying dead in her living room, the hatchet used to kill her by her bloody head. At 9:42 in the morning.

There was a list of people Benny had talked to. No one knew much at all. Maddy had been seen the afternoon before, about three, out in her flower beds digging away. By a rancher who had come in to get a part from a friend who lived on the other side of Cooper. The rancher and his friend had met at the bar and had "a few beers" and then the rancher had gone back home.

About three.

No one had seen her after that.

So.

Du Pré looked at the stuff from the state, the Medical Examiner.

Maddy had died instantly from the blow to her head; the blade of the hatchet had smashed through her skull and compressed her brain. There wasn't much blood loss because she had died so quickly. Shock had probably stopped her heart.

She had been dead, the ME said, about twelve hours when Benny found her, for there were fresh botfly eggs on her which had not begun to hatch. The botflies flew only in daylight, and if she had died the night before when the sun was up the eggs would have either hatched or been about ready to.

Du Pré skipped the dry recounting of the inventory of Maddy's parts. He looked at the examination transcript.

She had a bruise on her chin, one that seemed to have come from a small protruding object. She could have fallen and hit her chin on something. A bolt head. The blunt end of a stake.

Or somebody could have hit her, ring on their hand, Du Pré thought.

The ME had thought of that, too, and if it was a ring it was one with a flat square stone in it.

That was all.

The evidence gathered seemed all to belong to her, hair and fibers matched the house and Maddy, there were no other kinds of hair, or strange fibers. No fingerprints. No nothing.

Nothing at all.

Whoever had killed her had hit her and walked out the door and never touched a thing but the hatchet handle, and that was rubber and held nothing at all on its surface. It was fairly new, sold by a hardware chain.

There were no footprints that fitted anyone but Maddy.

Du Pré finished his drink. He took the empty glass back to the bar and nodded to the woman and walked back up the street to the Sheriff's office.

Benny was at his desk, frowning at the papers.

"Maybe I have the key?" said Du Pré "Me, I think that I will sleep out there tonight. Outside, got my bedroll with me."

Benny took a small manila envelope from a drawer and handed it to Du Pré.

"One of the technicians allowed as how a murderer always leaves something at the scene," said Benny, "and then the guy said, 'But we don't always find it.'"

Du Pré nodded.

"Hope your dreams are good," said Benny. "Mine ain't been worth shit since I found her."

CHAPTER 7

"This is ver' good thinking, Du Pré," said Madelaine. "You will go and sleep, the lawn out back, no car around, so the guy who kill her comes back he can hit you, the head, with the hatchet and then I got an old dead crazy woman and an old dead Du Pré. I like how you think, yes."

She smiled at him.

It was cooler now than the nights had been and there had been a little bit of lightning high in the Wolf Mountains. The clouds were gone and the sky was velvet black and the stars glittered. A wind had come up at sunset and cleared some of the smoke away.

Fires out west are not burning so bad maybe today, Du Pré thought.

Madelaine turned in the drive and the lights shone on the yellow house. She drove up to the Oldsmobile and stopped. She kissed Du Pré.

He got his bedroll from the trunk of the cruiser and took out a cooler that had ice and water in it, and a little bag with some salty peanuts and a bottle of bourbon in it.

"I see you, the morning," said Du Pré.

"Ya," said Madelaine, "I come see you got a hatchet, your head."

He bent down and he kissed her and she smiled and backed out of the drive and drove off toward Toussaint.

Maybe they do come back, Du Pré thought, and maybe I hear them they come.

He carried his things around to the back of the house and he found a flat place and he unrolled the bedroll near one of the paper birches. The tree had been burned by the sun, even though it had plenty of water at the roots, and the leaves were dry and rattled when the breezes came.

"Goddamn dry," said Du Pré.

He found a folding chair and brought it over near his bedroll and set it up carefully and checked it. One had collapsed under him not long back and he had fallen and it had hurt.

Damn, I am getting old.

Du Pré mixed a drink and he rolled a smoke and lit it with the shepherd's lighter his daughter Maria had brought him from Spain. Just a flint and a steel wheel and a length of cotton rope. It worked well and he didn't have to buy lighter fluid.

He smoked and sipped his whiskey.

He yawned. Long day.

He had another drink and another cigarette. He pulled the soogan back on the bedroll and took off his boots and pants and shirt and he lay there looking up at the stars.

Bright green streaks across the sky. Meteor showers, we have them here, all the time, thick in late August.

Du Pré looked off toward the Wolf Mountains. There was no moon and so he could only tell that they were there, a little blacker than the night sky overhead.

The little ditch gurgled and the water chuckled from time to time.

A soothing sound.

Du Pré closed his eyes and slept.

He woke suddenly.

He was dreaming that he had heard voices.

"I'm scared, Willie," said a girl. "This is creepy. An old lady was murdered here, you know, I want to go."

"Nah," said Willie. "A minute. I want to look in the windows."

They were around at the side of the house.

Du Pré could see a little glow, the beam from the flashlight the boy must be carrying.

"Willie!" said the girl.

"Beth, it's all right," said Willie. "I made a bet and I got to do this."

The flashlight moved toward the back of the house and Du Pré.

A tall boy peered in the kitchen window, looking carefully and playing the light around.

Du Pré sighed.

The boy never looked anywhere but in the house.

He edged across the back of the place.

He looked in the little frosted window of the bathroom.

He went on.

"Willie!" said the girl. "I think there's somebody coming! We have to go!"

"Keep an eye on 'em," said Willie. "Let me know they get close."

Du Pré shook his head.

Kids.

"Willie, it's probably the Sheriff," said the girl.

"Christ," said Willie, "you sure whine a lot."

Du Pré heard a door slam, a car door and a crunch as the tires went over the gravel.

He got up and pissed and went back to the pile of clothes by his bedroll. He got his makings and rolled a cigarette. He smoked it slowly and tossed the butt into the little irrigation ditch and crawled back into the bedroll.

He tossed and turned for a while, and then he began to sink down into sleep.

He had no dreams.

He woke up suddenly.

He had heard something.

Breaking glass.

Du Pré carefully slid out of the bedroll and reached for the flashlight in the little bag.

It wasn't there.

He got up on his hands and knees.

He shook his head.

I am dreaming of breaking glass, he thought.

He waited, tense.

The breeze rattled the leaves of the paper birch.

Du Pré turned his head, trying to hear carefully.

Something moved, a footstep maybe. Around the side of the house. Near that little shed.

Du Pré listened again but the wind was coming up and he couldn't hear well now.

Something? Nothing.

The grass had been carefully tended and he walked across it barefoot. He paused by the corner of the house and listened.

Something? Nothing?

The wind soughed.

Something creaked and Du Pré tensed.

The shed door moved a little.

God damn, Du Pré thought, I did not latch that well.

He waited a moment and then walked toward the shed door. It was only open about a foot. He pushed it to, and he turned.

He took the blow on his forehead and saw stars and fell back.

He woke feeling rain on his face.

"Du Pré!" said Madelaine. "Du Pré you can hear me yes!"

Du Pré screwed his eyes shut and he blinked. He felt sick to his stomach and he sat up rolling, gagging, and puking. He dry-heaved for a while, choking.

Madelaine knelt beside him. He felt cool wet cloth wiping his face.

"Got a big dent in your head there, Du Pré," she said. "I help you walk we get you to a doctor."

Madelaine pulled him to his feet and put his arm over her shoulder and walked quickly toward the cruiser. She was not a big woman but she was very strong. She held Du Pré while she pulled open the door and then she sat him on the seat and lifted his legs in. The window was down and Du Pré put his face out so if he puked again it would go outside.

Madelaine backed out to the road fast and put the cruiser in drive and punched the accelerator.

"You talk to me Du Pré I know you are not dead over there, eh?" she yelled over the rushing wind. "Tell me one your bullshit stories there, Du Pré."

Du Pré laughed and then he began to cough.

"Where you find me?" he said. "I am in my car, but why am I here?"

Madelaine looked over and she put her eyes back on the road.

"Somebody hit you damn hard. You are at Maddy Collins house, do you remember? Maddy Collins?"

Du Pré laughed and laughed. The light was dancing outside and everything had a crackling black border around it and it was all very, very funny.

Du Pré laughed and laughed and tears streamed down his face.

"Du Pré!" said Madelaine. "I am here you are all right."

She floored the accelerator.

Du Pré slumped down.

CHAPTER

8

Du Pré opened his eyes and saw a lot of little black dots on white.

He blinked a few times.

He inhaled.

He looked over at his left.

An IV bottle on a rolling rack.

"Fuck," said Du Pré.

"You makin' a habit of this," said Booger Tom. He was sitting in a chair by the bed. The old cowboy's drooping white mustaches touched his shirt collar.

"Shit," said Du Pré.

"Man oughta not stay in this damn place long," said Booger Tom. "I come in and that mean nurse had me by the throat said if I fed you any whiskey she'd scramble my sweetbreads and brains and eat 'em. I think she about meant it. Seems there's somethin' in that bottle drippin' into your arm ain't improved by whiskey."

Du Pré screwed his eyes shut tight.

Booger Tom had four lips and four mustaches now.

"Shit," said Du Pré.

"Yer vocabulary is comin' back," said Booger Tom. "Now you just rest, whilst I go and tell the nurse you's awake. She made me promise come tell her you did."

He went out the door.

The nurse soon came.

She held up one finger on her right hand in front of Du Pré's eyes.

"How many fingers?" she said.

"One," said Du Pré.

She moved the finger and watched his eyes. She took out a little flashlight and she looked at each of his pupils.

"Hooray," she said, "they're the same size. Good thing when they are. Means your brain isn't swelling."

"It could use some," said Booger Tom.

"Tell ya what," said the nurse, "you got a quarter? I will kill this old bastard for twenty-five cents."

"Take a dollar," said Du Pré. "Kill him four times. Make sure." His voice was cracked and his throat hurt.

"Madelaine's sleeping at my house," said the nurse. "I'll go call her now." She went off briskly.

Du Pré coughed and choked and he tried to sit up. Booger Tom stuck his hard old hand behind Du Pré and lifted him so he could breathe.

"Damn," said Booger Tom, "hit ya on the head, ya half-breed son of a bitch, shouldn't a hurt."

Du Pré nodded.

Booger Tom held a glass of water to Du Pré's lips. He sipped. It tasted of chlorine and sulfur.

"Godawful water these parts," said Booger Tom. "Whiskey makes it a little better."

Du Pré slumped back.

The nurse came back in.

She checked Du Pré's pulse and blood pressure and she tapped his knees with a little triangular rubber hammer.

"Good," she said. "Good."

Booger Tom kept well out of her way.

"It's Monday," she said, "three-thirty in the morning. This old goat has been sitting here for three hours. You've been out cold for forty-eight. We were worried about swelling, but it looks good. The doctor will be in in a few minutes. You had seizures and damn near died on us. Whoever cracked you one meant business."

Du Pré blinked.

"Cracked me one?" he said.

"You may never remember having been hit or the events just before it," said the nurse. "You had a doozy of a concussion. Do you remember where you were?"

Du Pré thought.

Meteors streaking across the sky. He had been outside.

"Maddy's place," said Du Pré.

"Good," said the nurse. "Now, just sips of water. You can have a bite to eat as soon as the doctor sees you."

Du Pré looked at the little holes in the ceiling tiles.

He closed his eyes. A wrenching, splitting headache burst into his brain. He gasped.

Booger Tom was down the hall like a shot.

The nurse came back.

She bent over.

"Head?" she said.

"Yes," said Du Pré.

"It's a good sign. I can't give you anything, but as soon as the doctor sees you I will, and damn strong, too."

Du Pré nodded. The pain was coming in waves.

He lay back.

Footsteps.

A cool hand on his forehead, lips on his, faint musky perfume.

Madelaine.

"Hoo Du Pré," she said, "I am saying rosaries for you, lots of them. You be all right now."

Du Pré grimaced.

Someone came into the room.

Du Pré opened his eyes.

The doctor. He asked a few questions, tapped a few things, looked at Du Pré's eyes, and stood up.

"Let's get your headache gone," he said.

The nurse came in with a syringe and she stuck it quickly in a vein in Du Pré's arm and he felt warmth and then the pain dissolved.

"PRN," said the doctor. "Good going."

He went off, his lab coat swaying.

Madelaine came back. She smiled at Du Pré.

"Who hit me?" he said.

Madelaine put her palms up.

"Maybe the same guy kill Maddy," she said. "He sure hit you damn hard. Dent in your skull they pop out. I don't know how they do that, but they do."

Booger Tom was in the corner yawning.

"G'night," he said, and he trudged off.

"What am I hit with?" said Du Pré.

"One, those old nail pullers got the sliding handle," said Madelaine.

Jesus, Du Pré thought, they weigh ten pounds. Pop my skull like a grape.

"I come get you early, find you lying there, lot of blood, I toss water in your face, get you to the car. We get to Toussaint you are jerking and got your mouth open. I jam a roping glove in there so you don't bite your tongue. Helicopter is there, half an hour, they bring you here."

Du Pré nodded. The clinic.

"They got stuff here, give you, you are some better, so they don't fly you, Billings."

Du Pré nodded.

"Benny he look around?" he said.

Madelaine nodded.

"Nothing. He find a couple kids, were there earlier, the night, but they never saw you."

"I am at the whorehouse," said Du Pré.

"Oh, Du Pré," Madelaine cooed, "you get well so I can kill you, eh? What they got, the whorehouse, I don't give you?"

"I don't know," said Du Pré, "but maybe something."

She patted his hand.

"Full of shit," she said, "my Du Pré who I love."

"I don't remember some," said Du Pré. "Them kids they come, shine a flashlight, the windows, but I just lie there, my bedroll. Not worth scaring them even."

"They plenty scared now," said Madelaine. "Benny he yell at them a lot. They look all over, find the nail puller, but it don't got nothing on it. Like with Maddy there is nothing."

Du Pré nodded.

"Maybe the guy, kill Maddy," said Du Pré.

Madelaine nodded.

She held Du Pré's hand.

"There is something else, Du Pré," she said.

Du Pré looked at her.

"We get you here, you are going to be all right, I am here, Benny, everybody is worried. This is night before last. Nobody sees until it is too late, Maddy's house is burning. Fire gets into the field, everybody goes to fight it, they stop it. Put the fire out, Maddy's house. Wet it down good, look through what is left. Find a dog in it. Bad burned."

"Dog?"

"Somebody put a dog in the house, burn the house down, Du Pré," said Madelaine.

Du Pré shook his head.

41

CHAPTER 9

"Good, good," said Pidgeon. She was with the FBI and had called Du Pré at Susan Klein's bar.

Jesus, Du Pré thought, I tell her this old lady gets killed with a hatchet and her house gets burned couple nights later and I am hit on the head with ten pounds of cast iron and some dog, which is Gus, belongs to Susan Klein, nice old dog likes everybody, is burned up in the house.

Good, good.

Jesus.

"Got anything else," said Pidgeon, "anything at all you can think of? Was the old lady mutilated or raped? The dog?"

"Non," said Du Pré.

I am upset I say *non.*

"Think," said Pidgeon.

"He's real quiet," said Du Pré.

I don't hear him, he hit me damn hard. So hard last thing I

remember is the meteor shower. Kids coming to snoop, get the chills, like they are at a bad horror movie. Willie and Beth.

Some few things were coming back, between the headaches. Doctor says the headaches come and go a while, come less, go longer, I am lucky to be alive.

So me, I can live, this bad horror movie.

"Well," said Pidgeon, "right off I can tell you you got a classic sociopath there. Mean to animals and people and sets fires. So maybe he was abused as a kid. Learned that being mean gets him things. Now, there are a few possibilities. Could be a kid, just starting out. Though the dog should have been killed before the old lady if it was a kid. If it is a kid, and he's local, he will have had a lot of trouble in school and he will probably have quit or been thrown out. If it is an older guy, he probably has done more of this. He may have gone away from your patch a while, but there should be a police record on him. They get in trouble far enough to be suspected, but they almost never get in trouble far enough to be arrested and convicted. It's like they have these antennae, pick up vibrations or something. When they do get caught, it is damn near an accident. Cop happens by, headlights on, the guy is tossing body parts off the bridge or something. Other thing I suspect, me being fond of dopey theories, isn't something I'd say to a roomful of my peers. They are incredibly lucky. Ted Bundy killed maybe a hundred women, and he got arrested and tried and escaped and he ran and it wasn't until he got stopped in a stolen vehicle that it ended. He'd get on a suspect list and leave town. Like he saw the list. I figure about half these guys die of natural causes. Old age. Accidents. They never show up on the screen."

"Shit," said Du Pré.

"Yeah, shit," said Pidgeon. "Why I went into this, see if I could maybe do something about it. So far, a little. You have wandered into the worst badland in the human heart, Du Pré. There are plenty of others but this is the worst."

"I am all in the dark," said Du Pré, "why the guy don't kill me?"

Pidgeon was tapping something, a pen on her desk perhaps.

"The old woman was killed by one blow to the head?" she said.

"Yes," said Du Pré.

"Dog will have been, too, they look," said Pidgeon. "That's what he does. One whack. Now, there could be a lot of reasons he just does the one whack there, but the one that comes to mind is blood spray. One whack means no blood spray, and blood spray is evidence."

"Jesus," said Du Pré.

"Other thing," said Pidgeon, "is he could be really fastidious. So he hates the thought of being spattered, marked, clothes spotted. *Dirty*."

"OK," said Du Pré.

"But," said Pidgeon, "there's stuff don't fit, too. The dog. I don't like the dog *after* the old lady, in the burning house. The old lady should have been burned in the house. I don't like the fact that you are alive. No offense, but that doesn't fit the theory. Should be dead. Other thing is, I don't like three times. I really don't like that. Guys like these aren't *fools*. Going back there three times, once to kill the old lady, once to whack you, and once to burn up the house with the dog. Not to mention killing someone's dog attracts attention, usually—people are awful fond of their dogs. So call it four. That's a lot of thumps and matches for a few days in the same tiny town. Nope, I don't like it. Don't fit my theory. Don't fit, and nothing a Phud hates more'n having their Phud thesis ring the bullshit bell."

"Phud?" said Du Pré.

"P-H-D," said Pidgeon. "The old doctorate. To get one of those you have to grovel and cringe and beg several folks already got their Phuds. Folks who has got Phuds don't like the thought of there being a glut of Phuds."

Du Pré laughed.

"Laugh, damn you," said Pidgeon, "me, I sit here thinking on serial killers and other such fine folks. This could get worse. I could have to deal with the psych faculty at a leading university. I did that, get the Phud. I like serial killers better, come to think on it."

Du Pré snorted.

"So I call you maybe I got questions," said Du Pré.

"Any time," said Pidgeon. "How's the little monster Pallas doin'? Ripper blanches whenever I mention her name. So I mention it a lot."

"Special school she is going to," said Du Pré, "Minneapolis."

"Good," said Pidgeon, "I will talk to Ripper, let him know his intended is transferring here. Georgetown University, easy walking distance of the Jedgar Building. Jedgar must designed this his own self. It is perfectly hideous."

"Jedgar?" said Du Pré.

"J. Edgar Hoover," said Pidgeon, "our founding fascist."

"Oh," said Du Pré.

"Sooo . . . ," said Pidgeon, "I got some charmer in New York killin' whores. As if whores don't have enough problems already."

"Thanks," said Du Pré.

"Got a pencil?" said Pidgeon. "Go get one you don't."

Du Pré fetched one from the bar.

Pidgeon gave him her home phone number.

"You need me you call anytime," said Pidgeon. "How's Bart?"

"OK," said Du Pré, "blading a lot of firebreaks."

"He's a good guy," said Pidgeon. "Well, 'bye."

Du Pré went to the phone and put it back on the charging stand. He could walk around with this one, it had an aerial on it.

Modern times.

"How is that Pidgeon?" said Madelaine. She was beading a belt, with blue and yellow beads.

"Good," said Du Pré. "She say I should be dead."

"No," said Madelaine, "you should not be dead. Neither

should old Maddy be dead, or poor Gus. Kill a poor old dog. Nice old dog."

Du Pré nodded.

"So what she say?" said Madelaine.

"It is somebody abused as a kid," said Du Pré.

Madelaine nodded.

"Don't like dirt," said Du Pré.

Madelaine nodded.

"That is why he hits one time only, don't want to get blood, his clothes."

Madelaine nodded. She put a bead on her needle and watched it slide down the thread.

"But she say that everything was not right. Dog should have been killed first, then Maddy killed, her house burned."

Madelaine nodded.

"Sounds like these people got a union, got rules," said Du Pré.

Madelaine looked up.

"Non," she said.

Du Pré looked at her.

"Non," said Madelaine, going back to her beads. She poked around in the little shallow dish full of the blue ones.

Du Pré rolled a smoke.

He lit it.

"Non, what *non?"* he said.

"That Pidgeon she think same person do all of this, but I do not," said Madelaine. "I do not think that."

Du Pré looked at her.

Madelaine held up her needle and she put a bead on it.

"Three persons," she said. "One kill Maddy. One hit you. One kill the old dog, burn the house."

Du Pré smoked.

"OK," he said, "why you think that?"

"Murderer kills Maddy," said Madelaine, "scared kid hits you, he thinks you are the guy killed Maddy."

Du Pré nodded.

"Bad kid burns the house down, puts the dog in it," said Madelaine.

"Why kill the dog?" said Du Pré.

Madelaine looked at him.

"Anybody look at the dog?" she said.

"OK," said Du Pré.

CHAPTER 10

Willie and Beth were sweating. They fidgeted.

They were sitting on two miserably uncomfortable chairs in a conference room at the school.

Du Pré was looking at them. Not staring, just looking.

"We didn't do anything," said Beth. "We just went out there to look at the place. It was creepy."

Du Pré took his little pocketknife from his pants and opened the pen blade and began to clean his fingernails.

"I know you don't do nothing," he said. "I am there, I hear you two talking. You don't do nothing. Somebody hit me later, hit me damn hard, and you know who that was."

"Honest . . ." said Beth. She thought about that for a moment.

"Beth!" said Willie. "Don't be a rat!"

"You," said Du Pré, looking at him, "are watching bad TV. Kid like you is out there, I scare him maybe he hits me. Me, I do not care he hit me. I live. But he hit me hard enough I do not remember it, I do not remember maybe an hour before, some days after. He was there. Maybe he saw something. So I need to talk to him."

Willie looked mad. He was stupid and he didn't know what to do and it pissed him off.

"Justin," said Beth. "Justin Wyman."

Du Pré nodded.

"OK," he said, "thank you."

He left before Willie started bitching at Beth.

She is smarter than him. Too much smarter. She can run him OK but there is less there to run, she need, Du Pré thought.

Dumb shit.

Du Pré stuck his head in the principal's office. The secretary looked up.

"Justin Wyman," said Du Pré.

She looked at some charts on a clipboard, the kind that has arched steel posts on it.

"Down the hall there, third door on the right. Civics," said the secretary.

Du Pré nodded.

He went down the hall, knocked on the door.

A young woman teacher came to it and opened it.

"Yes?" she said.

"Justin Wyman," said Du Pré.

There was a crash and some chatter and Du Pré went around the teacher.

Justin Wyman was trying to slide out of the window, the sort that hinges in the center and swings open for fresh air. His weight made the window tip up.

Du Pré grabbed the JUSTIN on his cowboy belt and hauled him back in.

He was a big kid and he took a swing at Du Pré.

Du Pré slapped him.

"We talk," he said. He let go and turned around and walked past the teacher, who was dropmouthed, to the hall.

Justin followed along.

"Mr. Du Pré, I'm sorry," he said, "I . . ."

Du Pré nodded.

He motioned for the kid to follow him. They went out the front door of the school. Du Pré went to his cruiser and got in and Justin got in with him.

Du Pré rolled a smoke and offered it to Justin, who took it, smiling.

"You are there you see what?" said Du Pré. "You see me, you think I am what?"

"I didn't know," said Justin. "I was there and suddenly I saw you move. Your skin, I guess. White. So I ducked behind the door to the shed. The nail puller was hanging on the wall. I grabbed it and when you moved the door I swung it and ran."

Du Pré nodded.

"You are there, you are looking for what?" he said.

"Pokin' around," said Justin.

"Pret' late at night, kid be pokin' around," said Du Pré. "You got parents."

"My mother works nights," said Justin. "She's a practical nurse, she takes care of old Mrs. Pritchett six days a week. Six P.M. to six A.M."

Du Pré didn't bother to ask about Justin's father. He was someplace else.

Justin was whitefaced.

"I thought I'd killed you so I run," he said. "I didn't know what to do. I thought you was dead."

Du Pré nodded. He pointed to the bandage on his head.

"I am not dead but I get these bad headaches, makes me pissy. So who burned the place down?"

Justin looked innocent.

"Listen," said Du Pré, "your mother is not home, watching you, you got a car, balls, want trouble. You find trouble like flies, shit. So who burned down the fucking house. My head aches I am about to break yours maybe."

"I dunno," said Justin. He was scared now.

Du Pré tapped him on the shoulder so he would quit finding interesting things outside the window.

"Some mean bastard kills Susan Klein's nice old dog, Toussaint, puts that dog, the house, burns it down. Shit, what they are. Now, I am not personally mad, you, but I can get that way. I get that way, I go to Benny, say, arrest that little prick Justin Wyman, assault. You go, Deer Lodge, that one, we make sure, take it up the ass there a while . . ."

Justin turned white.

"Keifer," he said.

"Davy Keifer," said Du Pré, "that little bag of shit, he is in Pine Hills, there, I think."

Justin shook his head.

"He came back for a visit," he said. "Brought some dope and booze with him, we had a party out at that stock tank by Willard's."

Du Pré nodded. Kids drank beer at the stock tank. They had been drinking beer at the stock tank since about 1893.

Davy Keifer was a little mean bastard who got sent to the state school for boys for setting fires in cars and trucks. His father died drunk when Davy was eight or so. Mother still *was* drunk.

"Where did he go?" said Du Pré. "No shit."

"Billings," said Justin, "he hangs in Billings."

Du Pré nodded. He spat out the window.

"He is back maybe this weekend, bring some more that fine dope and some booze, yes?" said Du Pré.

Justin nodded.

"You are having good time, the dope, getting laid?"

Justin swallowed hard.

Du Pré grabbed him by the throat.

"I rip your head off maybe, shit down your windpipe. You lie me, now, you, he is back when?"

"Thursday night," said Justin. "He crashes in the old saloon."

Du Pré nodded. That was an old boarded-up building in

Cooper that sat out at the edge of town. Transients stayed there from time to time. There was a place in the back where you could park a car out of sight.

"He is bringing you that fine dope you are selling it, the school," said Du Pré.

Justin looked like he was going to cry.

"You are big shit," said Du Pré, "selling dope, they like that here."

"Some do," said Justin.

Du Pré looked off.

"You are eighteen now yes?" he said.

Justin nodded.

"I got set back a year. Fourth grade," he said. "Had to do it twice."

"You got busted, any?" said Du Pré.

"Beer," said Justin.

"Here is it, how it will be for you. You are going Billings, you are enlisting, the Army. You do that, I don't call Benny, say, Benny, I want to see Justin, Deer Lodge, taking it up the ass."

Justin looked at Du Pré.

"Uh," he said.

Du Pré started the cruiser.

Justin reached for the door handle.

"Non," said Du Pré.

"I got to go back to school," said Justin.

"Non," said Du Pré, "you are going, Billings."

"Now?" said Justin.

"Yes," said Du Pré, putting the cruiser in reverse, "I know the way, Billings."

CHAPTER
11

Davey Keifer spat at the big Highway Patrolman. McPhie looked at the mean little man.

"Keifer," said McPhie, "you are gonna grow old and gray in Deer Lodge Prison. You want to have teeth, chew that fine food they got there, mind your manners."

Keifer stared sullenly at the ground.

Du Pré stood back by Keifer's car. It was stolen. It had felony amounts of drugs in it. It had a handgun in it, too, and Keifer wasn't supposed to be around any of those.

And then there was Violet, who was voluptuous, barely dressed, scared shitless, and bawling, and, last but not least, thirteen years old.

McPhie opened the back door of his cruiser and shoved Keifer in, carefully banging Keifer's head on the doorframe. Keifer writhed and kicked in the backseat, his hands held behind him with steel.

"And now," said McPhie, "we can wait for a female deputy to come and take possession of dear sweet little Violet there."

They both thought of Officer Parker, a small, brave, blond cop who was dead of a virus given her by a cult.

McPhie looked at Du Pré.

"She was a good one," said McPhie. "Liked you, you know, other'n yer habit of driving seventy miles an hour over speed limits with enough whiskey in ya to embalm ya."

Keifer screamed a long string of unpleasant words.

"Shaddup ya little shit," said McPhie, "I done ya a favor. Ya burnt up Sheriff Benny Klein's dog and another ten miles you'd be his prisoner."

Du Pré rolled a smoke.

McPhie pulled a tailor-made filter tip out of his pocket.

"That was pretty good," said McPhie. "There I am, setting by the road there, ready to grab the next miscreant comes along, and here goes none other than Davy Keifer, who I do not know, in a hot new red car, which looks all right to me, as there are any number of greasy little shits driving hot cars . . . and then you start in ramming him. Ram him hard. So I think, well, Du Pré is not liking that red car a whole lot, which makes me curious, so away I go."

"Him probably have a gun," said Du Pré, "so I want him shook up some."

McPhie looked off at the red car upside down in the salt sage pasture.

"Yeah," he said, "good thing they were both wearin' seat belts."

Violet got out of the cruiser. She was sniffling.

"Hon," said McPhie, "I told you you have to stay in there."

"I got to pee!" bawled Violet.

"By the car there," said McPhie, "there's a good girl."

"I don't know what else to do," said Du Pré, "I cannot shoot him, don't want him shoot us."

"Well," said McPhie, "the defense dick'll make all sorts of noise about po-lice brutality and all, and how you violated good citizen Keifer's rights, there, but the shit he's got in that car, not to mention Violet, there . . . well, it don't look good."

Keifer was trying to kick out the back window.

"You got a goddamn cattle prod?" said McPhie.

Du Pré shook his head.

"Never got one when ya need one. We always get accused of zapping our prisoners with cattle prods. I'd like to be guilty, just the once."

Violet stood up, sniffling.

"I don't wanna be in there," she said.

"Honey," said McPhie, "you have to. You just have to. Now, I know that Keifer, there, isn't real nice right now, but he wasn't before, and you were riding happily along with him."

Violet bawled and bawled.

McPhie waited, patiently.

"Young lady," he said. "In the car. Now."

Violet got in the front seat.

Keifer's feet had quit pounding on the rear window.

Violet got back out.

"I think he's stuck," she said.

McPhie nodded. He opened the door. He reached in and poked Keifer somewhere. Keifer screamed and began to curse.

McPhie shut the door.

"I was concerned," said McPhie, "that he might be uncomfortable."

Keifer yelled and yelled.

"Whatcha hit him inna nuts for?" she said.

"Nuts?" said McPhie.

"Could I havva cigarette?" said Violet.

"Nope," said McPhie, "you gotta be eighteen. It's the law."

"Fuck," said Violet.

"Get back in the car," said McPhie, "or I will put you in the backseat with Davey there."

Violet got back in.

A siren sounded a long way off.

"Help is on the way," said McPhie.

"I maybe talk to Keifer," said Du Pré.

"Little while," said McPhie. "Be about ten people here, a few more minutes. Give it maybe three days. He will be very easy to find."

Du Pré sighed.

"Maybe now," he said.

McPhie looked at Du Pré.

"Important?" said McPhie.

Du Pré nodded.

"Soon's Violet's gone," McPhie said. "And . . ."

"You don't know nothing," said Du Pré.

McPhie nodded.

"Don't mark him up," said McPhie.

The siren got closer and then the car came over the hill and it slowed and set its flashers and strobes and two people got out, one man, one woman.

The woman walked briskly over to the passenger side of McPhie's car and she opened it and said something and Violet got out and the woman took her arm and marched her over to the other car and put her in the back.

It took about twenty seconds.

McPhie nodded to them.

The other Highway Patrolman shook his head. He went back to the cruiser and got in and they turned around and headed back the way they had come.

McPhie sauntered away, whistling.

There were more sirens now, far away but closing fast.

Du Pré opened the back door and grabbed Keifer by the hair and hauled him out and slammed him facedown on the trunk lid.

Du Pré took a small ziplock bag from his pocket.

It had a ring in it.

He put it in front of Keifer's face.

"My fuckin' ring," said Keifer.

"We find it, under the old lady," said Du Pré, "like maybe she fight you pull it off you don't notice."

Keifer shut his eyes.

"Motherfucker," he said.

"You are going, to the jail," said Du Pré, "they are going to give you, there, paper, pencils. You write down everything you do in Cooper and Toussaint. What you do, when you do it, who you see."

Keifer gulped.

"Man," he said, "I didn't have nothing to do with old lady Collins. I killed the dog because that cunt Susan Klein gave me so much shit when I was in her class."

Du Pré leaned over.

"You are dirt," he said, "shit, and here, Montana, we kill people, do it at the prison, you could be one there. She was a crazy old lady, but kill her with a hatchet, leave her to rot?"

"I didn't kill her," said Keifer.

"Ring says you did," said Du Pré.

"I can find out who did. I can do that. I can," said Keifer.

Du Pré nodded.

"Maybe," he said.

"I can do it," said Keifer.

"Maybe," said Du Pré.

The sirens were getting closer.

"You are going away, ver' long time," said Du Pré, "but they got that lethal injection there now."

Keifer shut his eyes.

"You motherfucker," he said.

Du Pré pulled him up and tossed him back in the car.

McPhie came back.

"Find out?" he said.

Du Pré shook his head.

"He is worthless," he said.

McPhie nodded.

The sirens were there.

CHAPTER 12

"Vukovich," said the man in the cheap rumpled suit. "Call me Vook. That's what everybody calls me. Vook. Drug Task Force. Call the Billings office, ask for Vook they'll put you right through."

He was sitting on a stool in the Toussaint Saloon at nine in the morning drinking very bad coffee.

He looked at Du Pré.

"So," he said, "you aren't a cop, you were a brand inspector but you don't do much of that anymore, and you shove guys like Keifer off the road so the Highway Patrol can play with them. I like this. I like it a lot. The boonies. Once I lived in the Big City. Sheee-cago. Then one day a voice says, 'Vook, go to the boonies,' and so I come to Montana. I don't know how to do much but be a cop, and we do have drugs in Shee-cago, 'cept more of them and nastier people to go with them, or we did, and so, me having all this ex-perience on my résumé, why, they said, 'Vook, you got talents. Go out and catch us some druggies.' "

Du Pré wondered why the man couldn't say what the hell it was he wanted.

He drank his red beer.

His head ached and he'd taken the pills but they hadn't kicked in yet.

"Your head ache?" said Vook. "Sorry, I gas on, the mornings. I could come back."

"It ache anyway," said Du Pré. "So what is it you want."

"How'd you tumble to Keifer, anyway?" he said.

Du Pré shrugged.

Vook took a toothpick out of his pocket. He peeled the plastic away. He stuck it in his mouth.

"Methamphetamine," he said, "it is burning up country peo-ple all over. Billings is the capital of it, state of Meth, all the northern Rockies. It kills people. Now, Keifer is a little scumbag and he's going away for a long, long time, no matter what that long-haired faggot lawyer he got says about Keifer's various civil liberties gettin' raped by you and McPhie. But Keifer was bringin' that stuff here to sell, and that means he had some local salespeople, and I want 'em. You got no idea how bad this stuff is and how bad it hurts people. It's some kinda holocaust goin' on out in the sagebrush where nobody thinks there is drugs at all."

Du Pré sipped his red beer.

"I was you," said Vook, "I'd have me a ditch. I ain't here give you shit. I just need to talk and you got a headache and that shit is still out there, the sagebrush."

Du Pré laughed. He went around behind the bar and he made himself a ditch and he drank about half of it and he came back.

"I checked you out," said Vook. "Du Pré is a good guy, they say, real good guy, runs on Bull Durham and bourbon and he pisses on the little laws but he's good about the big ones."

Madelaine came out of the kitchen with two platters of breakfast, ham and scrambled eggs and country fries and toast. She set them in front of Vook and Du Pré.

They ate and did not speak.

Vook had more coffee after breakfast.

"That little sacka puke Keifer is hangin' tough, and he don't tell me a lot, yet. He's stupid, and it'll take some time, him, to realize he'd better help me so's I can help him. Only name he come up with is Justin Wyman. I asked around. He's in the Army now. You do that?"

Du Pré nodded.

"Hope you didn't get fucked," said Vook. "He's kinda stupid, right?"

Du Pré nodded.

"He hit you, give you them headaches, and you get him off," said Vook. "You think he's not too bad a guy, right?"

Du Pré looked at the detective.

"Him," he said, "dumb kid. Maybe four years, the Army, he is not so dumb."

"But he didn't give you any more names. See, that's what we do in this, we get one and pull their toes and they give us names," said Vook.

"Not going, wreck his life, other kids'," said Du Pré. "They are young and not smart."

Vook nodded.

"OK," he said, "I dunno, all I talk to is that little shitbag Keifer."

Du Pré's headache was sinking down.

"Keifer," said Vook, "Keifer is a little weasel who come up here, be King Turd with the teenyboppers. He's stupid, and he's toast now, but, thing is, he got the stuff we caught him with on credit. There's somebody up here, somebody local, dealing meth. Guy gave Keifer the credit, he's fucking with your local guy. That's the guy I want."

Du Pré looked at Vook.

"Here?" he said.

"Everywhere," said Vook. "I get this all the time. 'What? Here? In deepest Montana, where it is always 1888?' Yeah, here."

Du Pré looked at the bottles behind the bar.

Jesus Christ.

"Tell you a way to spot some a this," said Vook. "One way, you got say a couple, youngish, they used to come here, see the neighbors, maybe dance, Saturday night, maybe have a few drinks. They don't come no more. They ain't coming to church neither. When they do come to town to get groceries they don't get many, 'cause they don't eat much no more. Light hurts their eyes, so they wear real dark glasses, and they do what they got to do at night, they can."

Du Pré sighed.

Vook, he knows, stuff I don't know.

He is right.

Who I know, used to come and listen, fiddling, does not now?

Madelaine came out of the kitchen. She poured coffee for herself and she waved the pot at Vook, who shook his head.

"He is thinking we have drugs here," said Du Pré.

Madelaine nodded.

"Got 'em everywhere, Du Pré," she said.

"That methamphetamine," said Du Pré.

Madelaine nodded.

Vook said again what he had just said to Du Pré.

Madelaine nodded.

"What is this?" said Du Pré.

"I am here, the bar," said Madelaine, "so pretty much every-body come here, you know, see each other, maybe even they don't drink, religious."

Vook nodded.

"So I see a lot," said Madelaine.

"This is awful," said Vook, "I know. I see it alla time. Tears peo-

61

ple up awful. Your friends, your neighbors. But there's gotta be one guy sellin' here, and he don't use what he sells. He just takes the money. Him, I want. He's killin' people."

Madelaine nodded.

"Way to find 'em, too," said Vook, "I mean the ones that are messed up with this shit—they put foil on their windows. Keep out the light. So you drive along, see a house, windows flash silver, well, it ain't a good sign."

Madelaine nodded.

"The old lady," said Vook, "Collins? One of these guys on that stuff coulda gone there, rob her, panicked, hit her, forgot why he come and run. It could be that, maybe. Probably is."

Du Pré thought of the eight hundred dollars Maddy had.

Easy to find.

Somebody sick on this methamphetamine come, hit her with a hatchet, run he is scared?

"I just got here," said Vook, "I stick out like a fish in a tree, you know, so it saves time maybe you do it. Benny Klein he is a good guy, I hear. These people are your neighbors. Maybe you can get a couple of them, go in for treatment, get well. They got to get the shit from somebody. It's him I want."

Madelaine sighed. She went off toward the kitchen and she was gone for three or four minutes and she came back.

She had a cup of tea.

"Well," said Vook, taking out a five-dollar bill, "good chow. I hope this is enough, all I got on me."

He put it down.

Madelaine nodded.

"I see this all the time," said Vook. "Look, I ain't after the sick people 'less they did crimes, you know. Them I don't feel mad at. I want the sellers. Now, ma'am, I know you know some a who I was talkin' about there, and I am beating it outta here now. You do what you think is best."

Madelaine looked at Du Pré.

"I want the seller, though," said Vook. "I'll be back, two days, to get 'em."

Madelaine looked sad.

Vook walked across the old wood floor to the door and went out, and soon his car started.

Madelaine patted Du Pré's hand.

CHAPTER
13

"Well, fuck me runnin'," said Pidgeon. "Tell ya what. I'll come there and tend bar and Madelaine can come here and sweat. You know what the last day of August is like in Washington? I could get to like cactus."

Du Pré laughed.

"You don't know here," he said.

"Maybe," said Pidgeon, "maybe. Now, you say the guy that hit you on the head, he was just a kid and you got him in the Army. OK. He admitted it to you?"

"Yah," said Du Pré.

"And the guy burned the house and the dog did, too?" said Pidgeon.

"Yah," said Du Pré.

"And then this guy Vook said Maddy Collins was killed by a speed freak who panicked."

"He say maybe that," said Du Pré.

"Lemme see I got this," said Pidgeon. "Guy goes to Maddy's, opens the front door, which is unlocked, of course, old ladies always leave them unlocked, and then Maddy comes out of the back of the house and he panics."

"Yah," said Du Pré.

"Ooooh-kay," said Pidgeon. "Now this guy's brain is all fried by speed. Case you didn't know it, speed does a real number on basic thought processes. Anyway, he is there, and he gets freaked, and so he picks up the hatchet Maddy always leaves buried in the walnut table because she uses it to spread butter on her scones, and he whacks her once with the hatchet, blade first, so hard it goes four or five inches into her brain. Then this addled speed freak, touching nothing, and he must have been wearing latex gloves, goes out the door and leaves it open. Why was the door left open, Du Pré?"

"So she would be found," said Du Pré.

"Well, well," said Pidgeon. "Now, anything wrong with the picture I just painted?"

"The hatchet," said Du Pré.

"Look," said Pidgeon, "what I gave you was a guess. That's all, and I was right some and wrong some. Told you the dog bothered me, and a couple other things. But there is one thing I can tell ya. Maddy was killed by somebody who wanted to kill her and who planned it well and who went there with the hatchet. Now, I don't know a lot about how you live out there, but, well, I went camping with my father a lot. He said hatchets were dangerous toys. Handles too short, heads too heavy, only good for hurting yourself with."

"Yah," said Du Pré.

Hatchets were worthless and no one split kindling with them. You used an ax, it was safe and easier.

"The guy you put in the Army could've killed Maddy," said Pidgeon.

"No," said Du Pré.

"Du Pré," said Pidgeon, "you know something."

"No," said Du Pré, "I am not keeping back."

"You don't know it but you do," said Pidgeon.

"You are sounding like Benetsee," said Du Pré.

"Go see him," said Pidgeon. "That's highly scientific advice."

"This is a bad guy," said Du Pré.

"Very bad guy," said Pidgeon. "Now, when I said it could be this Justin Wyman, I said that because these people are incredible actors. They don't have personalities of their own. They have to borrow 'em. They aren't really human. They are damn hard to catch. Now, it could be Wyman, or not. I don't know. One way to tell, though."

Du Pré waited.

"If he writes you a lot, thanking you for getting him into the Army which he loves," said Pidgeon.

"I do not understand," said Du Pré.

"Put these guys in prison," said Pidgeon, "they shine like stars in all the counseling programs. Easy way to spot 'em for a shrink is, when he shows up, these guys are right there, all charm and oil, and doing better than anyone else. They are real charming. They don't get lines in their faces, either."

"Huh?" said Du Pré.

"No conscience, no guilt, no lines," said Pidgeon.

"Justin, him too dumb," said Du Pré.

"Check," said Pidgeon. "Get the school records. See about his IQ. It may be low or it may be very high, but the thing is his schoolwork won't match his numbers there."

"Ah," said Du Pré.

"OK," said Pidgeon, "call me later. When you know more. And you just may have gotten Maddy Collins's murderer out of town."

Du Pré hung up.

He sighed and he picked up the coffee cup. He was sitting in Madelaine's kitchen.

She was finishing her shower and Du Pré heard the water turn off.

I am confused. Dope here, bad dope. Don't know I did the right thing, Wyman.

Benetsee.

Du Pré got up and went outside and looked off toward the Wolf Mountains. The air was murky from the fires to the west. He looked west.

There was a black line low on the horizon.

Shit, it is that dry lightning cloud, Du Pré thought.

He shook his head and rolled a smoke and he sat at the table he made for Madelaine the first summer they were seeing each other.

And now we go, see neighbors in trouble.

Madelaine came out, dressed, her long black and silver hair wound up in a towel.

Du Pré rolled her a smoke.

She took the one long drag she liked and gave it back to him.

She sat down.

"Well," she said, "we got to go and see them, hope we can talk them, going down to Billings."

The Bergers. Old ranching family, the one son running the old place, parents both dead, both Paul Berger and his wife, Peggy, had been coming to hear Du Pré for years. They had a daughter, twelve, who was in school here in Toussaint, the little two-room school.

Madelaine had known instantly who was in trouble.

So she and Du Pré and Father Van Den Heuvel were going out to the Berger place, to try and talk with them.

Foil on the windows.

The daughter getting more pale and drawn and sad each day.

School had just started and in the spring she had been happy and smiling.

Ranching is tough work, Du Pré thought, take drugs, you can do more work, a while.

A while.

Madelaine unwound the towel and let her gleaming wet hair

fall forward. She sat with her head down close to her knees and she rubbed the towel and then put it aside and got a fresh one and then began to brush out her hair.

"You know, Du Pré," she said, "we got problems, you got, your appendix bust, because you are a dumb-shit cowboy and you won't go, the hospital, till you are carried, and our kids, they have a little trouble and we don't have much money, long time, but we don't got problems like Bergers do. God, He been very good to us."

Du Pré nodded.

"So," said Madelaine, "we maybe help God along here some, them Bergers."

Du Pré nodded.

The Bergers were cheerful hardworking people. They had come to listen to Du Pré, and then, maybe a year ago, they had stopped.

Now, they weren't seen.

Peggy Berger would drive the daughter, Laurie, to the store and Laurie did the shopping while her mother sat in the pickup, chain-smoking.

Son of a bitch, Du Pré thought, there is bad stuff in the world.

Fucking little Keifer.

Fucking bastard who is selling, his neighbors.

"You give him to that Vook," said Madelaine. "Du Pré your brain it is shouting at me."

A car pulled in and stopped out front.

"Father Van Den Heuvel," said Madelaine.

The big clumsy Belgian priest came around the corner of the house.

He looked sad.

He was going to try to help troubled people, and he wished all the trouble in the world gone.

68

CHAPTER
14

"Moved up here from California five years ago," said Vook. He was sitting in Benny Klein's cruiser. It was dark out, an hour or so before dawn.

They were one of six cars lined up just over the hill from a small ranch owned by a couple named Biedermann.

The other cars held Task Force people and DEA agents.

Four of the people were in uncomfortable moon suits. The chemicals in crank labs were highly toxic, and those who ran them weren't above booby-trapping their works.

The radio was silent. They might have scanners in the house.

There was a tap on the window.

Vook rolled it down.

"Five," said the man in the black jumpsuit and body armor.

"We will be far behind you," said Vook, "matter of fact, why don't you call when it's over."

"Vook," said the man, "cut the crap. It's all we can do to keep from gettin' trampled by your fat Polack feet, you wantin' to get in there so bad, get them bad guys, Vook."

"I said I was sorry," said Vook.

"Yeah," said the man, "you said that, you knocked me down and put your fat Polack hoof between my shoulder blades, you were passin' by. Now *this* time, Vook, we got orders to shoot ya ya get outta the car before one of us comes back *out* of the house. Vook. Give me a fuckin' excuse."

Du Pré laughed.

Vook looked pained. "OK OK OK," he said.

"Shoot to fuckin' *kill*," said the man. "They maybe got a machine gun in there but it's less dangerous than your fat Polack feet."

"Awright," said Vook,

The man walked away.

"Friend of yours?" said Benny.

"Yeah," said Vook, "guess he is. Well, I was goin' in and he was dorkin' around and maybe I *pushed* him just a little."

The cars passed Benny's cruiser one by one, all dark, all well-tuned, all silent.

A Montana Power crew was at the pole, out of sight of the ranch house, waiting to cut the electricity off to the second. The lineman was by the transformer.

"Ya never know," said Vook. "We had guys killed, Chicago, went in places, they didn't know the scum in there was ready for 'em. We don't take no chances now."

"Good," said Benny. He was a gentle man and he hated violence.

"Minute it's go," said Vook, "there'll be a lotta light there, and we can pull up far enough to see."

Benny started the cruiser.

"Two minutes," said Vook.

One minute.

There was a brief blue flash at the power pole and then lights came on where the ranch house was, and Benny eased forward to where they could see.

The cop cars screeched up to the house; men got out and bashed open the door and were inside in ten seconds.

Others went around the sides.

Others checked outbuildings.

Du Pré rolled a smoke and lit it.

They waited; it seemed like a long time but it wasn't.

Four people stumbled out, two of them naked and two wearing only underwear. Two men, two women. The women covered their breasts. Then a cop in riot gear pointed a shotgun at them and they all lay down and crossed their wrists behind their backs.

"We can go down now," said Vook.

Benny hesitated.

"They won't shoot *you*," said Vook. "It's just me they don't like. Polacks."

Benny drove forward and turned and went down the driveway. The little ranch house wasn't far away from the road and everything was going quite smoothly.

Benny parked back from the black cars.

Vook and Du Pré got out.

Benny didn't.

A huge cop came out carrying a small child, and then another with another kid.

The children turned their eyes away from the blazing lights. They buried their faces in the flak jackets.

"Shit," said Vook, "that's the worst. They got kids, grow up with this. Had a couple got cancer from the chemicals, while ago, they're both dead now."

The four people down on the ground were handcuffed and silent, but the big cop with the shotgun kept his gun to hand.

Du Pré' could see light touching the crowns of the Wolf Mountains. The east was getting paler and day would soon be along.

He looked over at the barn. It was sagging and in bad repair.

Something flashed inside.

Du Pré stared.

Flames burst out of a window and then two cops ran out of the open sliding doors.

The barn blew up. It did not fly apart, but it was a mass of flame in seconds.

"Jesus!" said Du Pré, "Call 911. Get the fire people here."

He started to move toward the pump house and then he remembered that the power was off.

The barn roared and swirls of sparks went up hundreds of feet and some fell out in the dry grass in the pastures. The grass hadn't been grazed and it was thick and barely wet with dew.

Three minutes later several spot fires were growing toward one another.

Benny was on the radio, yelling.

The spot fires got together and then there was a sudden wind that made the flames dance and run.

To the line of dry brush along the little creek.

The ranch was a mile or so from the Wolf Mountains.

Du Pré looked inside the cab of a pickup. The keys were in the ignition. He started it and he drove off toward the mountains. He swerved around the flaming grass in the pasture and headed on to the line of brush on the creek.

There was a shovel sticking up, handle down, in one of the stake holes.

Du Pré looked for a place where he might slow the fire. There was a wet place, filled with dead cattails, but no tag or willows. He got to it and he began to bash away at the cattails. The little swamp was very dry and the cattails tough.

The fire was moving right up the brush line.

Du Pré got out of the way just before the flames set the cattails alight. They burned swiftly. A southwest wind had come up and it shoved the flames along toward the foothills of the Wolf Mountains.

Du Pré sighed. He threw the shovel down and he trudged back to the ranch house.

A siren sounded far off, too far now to make any difference. The tanks were small on the trucks and the fire growing and there was not enough water in the little creek to pump from it.

He went to Benny, who was standing by the cruiser.

"Shit," said Benny.

Du Pré nodded.

The low flanks of the Wolf Mountains had burned in 1908, and afterward lodgepole pine had grown there, and lodgepole didn't live that long. There were hundreds of thousands of tons of fuel on the flanks of the mountains.

"I tried to get a plane," said Benny. "They're all over in the western part of the state."

Du Pré nodded.

The fire was accelerating, eating the brush along the creek faster and faster, and the grass was exploding and running ahead of that.

"They will burn now," said Du Pré.

"Maybe," said Benny.

The fire truck pulled in and the driver went right through a fence on his way to the flames.

But it was too far and the fire too big.

The fire truck stopped.

Benny looked over to the east, toward the south flanks of the Wolf Mountains.

"Shit," he said, "look at that."

A column of white smoke was rising, billowing up.

Du Pré squinted.

"We better go there," said Benny.

He and Du Pré ran for the cruiser.

CHAPTER
15

Du Pré and Benny got as close as they could to the fire, a trail-head used by packers taking strings back into the Wolf Mountains Wilderness. There were a dozen pickups there already. Two late arrivals were unloading off-road bikes. They had axes and Pulaskis strapped on the backs of the motorcycles. The two men waved at Du Pré and Benny and started the bikes and headed up a steep trail toward the smoke column.

"We can't do much," said Benny.

Du Pré nodded.

He stepped back so he could see farther down the smoke column. It was whitish and thick.

"You ever see smoke like that?" he said to Benny.

Benny stared at it a while.

"No," he said. "There's something isn't right about it."

A huge popping. The sound was less an explosion than a rattle of bangs.

"What the fuck was that?" said Benny.

Du Pré shook his head.

He heard an airplane and he turned and saw an old Liberator bomber lumbering toward the smoke column. The pilot banked and circled a hundred and eight degrees and then he went out of sight behind the treetops.

The Liberator appeared again, climbing and banking away from the mountains.

Du Pré laughed.

Long branches flapped from the wheels.

The pilot headed south.

They backed away and looked up again. The smoke column was broken now and not so thick and white.

"I'll be damned," said Benny, "that's about the first time the government ever did something right and on time, too."

They laughed. Du Pré pulled out his sack of Bull Durham and it slipped out of his fingers. He bent over to pick it up, still laughing, but Benny suddenly stopped.

"Oh . . . my . . . God," he said.

Du Pré grabbed the tobacco and stood back up and looked where Benny's eyes led.

A man was walking very slowly down the hill, stopping every few steps.

He was entirely black and flaps of his clothes hung from his legs and his arms and chest.

Du Pré started moving toward the man.

His eyes were bloodred in his black face, which had flaps of black material hanging from it, too.

It was his skin.

He came on, stiffly, a Burnt Man.

Du Pré had no idea who he was. A neighbor.

The Burnt Man walked down the last of the path, and he stepped onto the flat gravel pan of the trailhead. He walked on, seeming to look very far off, with his bloodred eyes. His lips were shrunk away from his white teeth.

Benny ran to the cruiser and he got the first-aid kit from the trunk and he carried it toward the Burnt Man. The man was walking, slowly, a step, a pause, a step, a pause.

"We're gonna help you," said Benny. He set down the aluminum case with the first-aid stuff in it and he stood in front of the Burnt Man, who stepped again and who paused.

"Stop," said Benny. "We're gonna help you."

The Burnt Man took another step.

Du Pré went to Benny.

They stared at the Burnt Man.

He took another step and he paused.

Benny was only a foot away from him.

The Burnt Man stood. His gloves were still on his hands, his skin hung down in black sheets.

The fire on the mountain suddenly roared and the smoke column rose thick.

It was getting darker.

Du Pré glanced up at the sky. Thick boiling gray clouds were moving swiftly past.

The Burnt Man stood, a foot from Benny, whose eyes were wide in horror.

"Fella," said Benny, "let me help you lie down and we'll get to work on you."

The Burnt Man stood there.

"Sit down, please," said Benny. He raised up his hands.

The Burnt Man grabbed Benny's revolver and he turned and he put the barrel in his mouth and he pulled the trigger and a spume of bone and brains splattered Benny.

"Oh my God my God my God," said Benny, backing away.

The Burnt Man fell slowly. He toppled finally, and lay still.

"Oh my God oh my God," said Benny.

"Du Pré!" shouted somebody. Du Pré turned toward the voice. Men came out of the trees in the east. Du Pré counted. Eleven.

They were dirty and smeared with black but seemed all right.

"Lou's up there," said one. They were so black Du Pré couldn't tell who he was, but the voice was familiar.

"How many went up?" said Du Pré.

Lou. Lou. Dykstra? The family . . . they had a place down below.

"Eleven," said the man.

"Twelve," said a man behind him. "There's eleven of us now."

"We got to go up and find Lou," said the first blackened man.

"He's here," said Du Pré.

"Lou!" the man screamed. He ran forward. He fell to his knees and looked at the charred corpse.

He grabbed handfuls of earth and threw them impotently at a rock.

The sooty men gathered around the dead Burnt Man.

"Jesus Christ," said one, very softly.

The kneeling man began to sob.

"What happened?" said Du Pré to the man nearest him.

"We run up there, and the fire was small, not spread much," said the man, "so we started workin' it, and Lou saw something smoldering up the hill and he went off to get it 'fore it blew up. But then the one we was workin' on, there was these poppings and it blew up. I was looking at what was near me. We were in a real bad place, up against one of those rock spurs. We all ran, downhill, got around the spur 'fore the fire got to it. We didn't see Lou after that, hoped he'd run west, gone down that little crick over there."

Another man had been looking at the two of them talking and he had come over.

"I was closer to Lou," he said. "Ours got hotter and I looked up once and there was this big flame, big red and yellow flame where I last saw him. It wasn't wood done that. It was gasoline."

The man Du Pré was talking to nodded.

"Thought I smelled it," he said. "Couldn't be sure, coulda been turpentine, you know how that pitch stinks."

"Lou just walk down here and die?" said the first man.

Du Pré shook his head.

"Got Benny's gun, stuck it in his mouth," he said.

The men nodded.

"Way he's burned, can't blame him," said the first man. "Take him three weeks he let the docs at him."

"God," said the other man. "Jesus. That's his ribs showin' there."

The storm overhead rumbled and lightning crashed nearby, close enough to deafen everyone. They looked at one another and spoke but made no more noise than a tankful of guppies. Mouths moved.

Lightning crashed all over, and a wind rose, but there was no hint of moisture at all.

Then fat drops fell, splacking on to the gravel. They stopped.

"Christ," said the nearest man, his voice sounding as though it was under water, "that's the show. There'll be hundreds of fires up there now."

Benny was trudging back to the Burnt Man with a blanket he had gotten from his cruiser.

He shook it out and was going to cover the blackened corpse but the brother was keening and throwing dirt.

Benny stood, holding the blanket's folds.

"Fellas," said a voice, "we'd best get outta here. There's a lot of old dead lodgepole below us."

Men moved toward their pickups.

Two husky sooty men picked up the brother and put him in the backseat of a crew cab.

Du Pré went to Benny.

"Come on, Benny," he said, taking the blanket and putting it over the corpse. "We can't do nothing."

CHAPTER 18

Du Pré and Madelaine and many other people stood out back of the Toussaint Saloon, looking at the mountains burning. The fires spread across the whole range, a cleft here, a mountainside there, blazing red. The clouds of smoke reflected the flames below.

A yellow gout of flame shot up.

Burning tree trunks were tossed long distances by the firestorm.

"We get a wind," said Madelaine, "nothing will be missed, there, Du Pré.

Du Pré nodded.

Nineteen-ten. I remember Grandpère Du Pré speak of that 1910. He is in a logging camp, Cabinet Mountains. They don't got telephones yet. See this pink glow to the west. All the horizon, pink.

Then they hear the fires.

Sound like trains coming.

They go out to cut a fire line, stop this fire.

"It is pink," said Grandpère, "and then it is salmon, and then it is red. Then is this big wind, pushing. Then we see it. Whole ocean of fire, coming to us. We run. Fire, it runs faster. Crew boss, he sees this mine, shaft goes into the mountain. He say, We go in there. One man shoot himself, afraid to burn. I got wife, babies, I can't die yet, they starve, I go in the mine. We are there all night. We lie in the water, breathe slow. Finally, the morning, the crew boss, he say he go look. He come back, say we go now, we walk back to the camp, it is not there. There is this burned bear, crying, foreman, he shoots him. We walk on. We walk all day, no water, it is all full of ashes. Pass deer, all black, elk, all black. Finally we come, Libby, it is still there, we get water.

"But everything it is ashes. One night, August 20, 1910. Nineteen-ten. Me, I never forget, 1910."

I know other old men, they say, *1910,* they look empty in their eyes.

Wind come up now, the Wolf Mountains, they will burn.

Forest Service firefighters had come that morning, and they had set up camp at the foothills, and they were fighting. In daylight there were helicopters and airplanes and big-bladed tractors cutting fire lines.

At night everyone pulled back.

"Christ," said Booger Tom, "I gone up there that fire camp and they had a leetle bit a wind kick up and they was all just setting there. That ain't no way to fight fire. You got to get in there and beat it. Goddamn government, anyway."

Du Pré laughed. The old cowboy held to the code. Any cowboy who wouldn't charge hell with one bucket of water wasn't worth spit.

"It is not worth somebody dying," said Madelaine, "them mountain, they burn they always burn. These silly people come here, don't want that logging, don't want anything touching the forests, I say, yes, it will be along, you know, touch that forest pret' good."

Du Pré laughed.

"Worse'n that, Coley was up there with his brother, got their Cats and they's cuttin' breaks on their own land, Forest Service prick tells them they can't, they ain't *trained*."

Du Pré laughed.

"Coley ain't got time for that crap, so he acts like he can't hear and he keeps on, feller finally parks his Forest Service Chevy Suburban in front of Coley."

Booger Tom had more beer from his mug.

"Coley's bearin' down on this here Suburban and the fool in it thinks Coley's too chicken to plow him away. Sure enough, Coley lifts that big damn blade up. Puts it down so gentle it don't scratch the paint on the roof of the goddamn thing, and then he lets that blade down a notch. Course, it weighs maybe eight tons. Roof starts comin' down on the government prick. Soon's Coley sees him scamperin' away he flattens the rig and then he shoves it on out to the county road. All the damn time the fool is a-hoppin' up and down screamin'. Coley finally tol' him get the hell off his property and when the feller wouldn't Coley got tired a his yappin' and busted his jaw. *Then* he left. I think Coley'n look forward to no end of trouble there."

Du Pré laughed.

There were ranchers who had small logging operations and good equipment and they sat idle. They knew the country much better than the men the Forest Service had brought.

"Same shit," said Madelaine, "they are the big federal guys, like the FBI, come in, local people we are dumb shits."

A swirl of fire exploded up from behind a mountain, a curtain of red. The mountain was black.

"So," said Du Pré.

"Take me, that Benetsee," said Madelaine, "I don't know, me, I just know we need to see him."

They went to Du Pré's cruiser and they drove off to the bench road and up the long hill.

There was a Forest Service roadblock there.

ROAD CLOSED RESIDENTS ONLY, said a sign, black letters on a blaze orange card.

Two Forest Service cops, gunbelts, with handcuffs and mirrored sunglasses, stood by a green Forest Service truck with police lights on a bar on the top.

They stood in the way.

Du Pré got out.

"Residents only," said one of the men.

They looked at Du Pré.

"I am going, see my grandfather," said Du Pré.

The two Forest Service men looked at each other.

"Can't let you through," said one. "Fire danger is too high."

Madelaine came out of the car running, her eyes blazing.

"You sons of bitches get your fat asses out, the road, now, we will go see Granpère you dumb shits now!" she yelled.

She was small but so mad the cops backed away from her.

Du Pré shook his head and walked back to the cruiser and got in and flipped on his light bar.

He pulled up to where Madelaine was chewing out the Forest Service cops. He rolled his window down.

"Madelaine!" he said. "You do not have, kill them tonight. Come on, we go now!"

Du Pré sighed. Madelaine was still cussing out the cops.

He got out and took her arm and tugged her back to the car and he put her in the backseat and he got in and drove past the gaping cops.

Madelaine could cuss good as any cowboy.

"I am not liking them motherfuckers," said Madelaine. "Get them a shovel, damn it, send them, fight the fire. Somebody is getting killed, Du Pré, they are that stupid."

"Yah," said Du Pré.

"Go on a rancher's land tell him he can't save his own grass one of these people get shot."

"Yah," said Du Pré.

"Goddamn mountains been burning last million years so let them burn. We don't need their damn help," said Madelaine.

"Yah," said Du Pré.

Madelaine slid over the seat.

She rolled down the window. The smell of burning pine came in, and smoke, and grass ashes.

Du Pré got to Benetsee's driveway and looked up it and saw another Forest Service cop car there, four-wheel drive.

"Oh, shit," said Du Pré.

He roared up to the cabin and he stopped his cruiser and he got out and he ran around past the woodpile to the path that led down to the sweat lodge and the creek.

He saw flashlights.

"You!" said Du Pré. "What are you doing?"

A light played on Du Pré's face.

"Do you live here, sir," said a voice.

"Non," said Du Pré.

"Somebody built a fire here, against the law, and we came and they went into the brush. Who lives here, sir?"

Du Pré laughed.

He looked at the lights.

"You better go now," he said.

The lights came closer.

"A crime has been committed, sir," said a voice from behind the flashlight. "The fire was over by that tent or whatever it is. No fires, that's the law."

"Go now," said Du Pré.

"If you interfere," said the voice, "you will be arrested."

A spotlight shot from the porch of the cabin, bright as a landing light on an aircraft.

The two Forest Service cops were blinded. They turned their faces away.

"You!" said Madelaine, "You put down, the guns, the lights now. You are trespassing! I got a shotgun, buckshot, I shoot you five seconds."

Du Pré laughed.

"Put the guns down I get you out of this," he said.

The two Forest Service cops took their weapons out of the holsters and put them on the ground.

Du Pré picked them up.

"Come along, you," he said.

CHAPTER
17

"This is a federal offense, buddy," said one of the Forest Service cops, "and kidnapping gets people decades in the joint."

Du Pré nodded. They were standing by the sweat lodge. The firepit where the rick had burned was still smoldering.

"You are so worried, fire," said Du Pré, "why you don't put this out?"

The two cops looked at the firepit.

"We did," said one of them.

Madelaine came and stood next to Du Pré.

"Why you are bothering this old man?" she said. "He don't let this fire away. It was not hurting anything."

"It could have started a fire," said the cop, "a major fire. There's a lot of fuel around here. Level Five restrictions."

"Bullshit," said Madelaine. "This is pret' wet here, the creek. It is not going anywhere."

"What you do?" said Du Pré. "Stop, take a piss, smell the smoke, drive up here, sirens, lights, guns out?"

"There was nobody here!" said the cop. "The goddamn fire was against the law!"

"Him here," said Du Pré.

"Hiding in the goddamn bushes," said the cop.

The fire in the pit began to grow and rise, purple and green flames rising slowly, caressing the air, sinking back down. A drum began to thump, back in the trees on the far side of the creek.

The fire grew very high, and it danced to the beat of the drum.

Voices. High, keening voices, singers, many of them, faint and far away. Ululations.

The cops looked at each other, scared; they had come to arrest someone and were now surrounded and unarmed.

The fire shrank back into the earth and all its light with it.

Benetsee stood there, old and bent and small. His black eyes twinkled merrily.

"Du Pré!" he said. "What is this? You come, bring guests!"

Du Pré rolled a smoke and he lit it and he carried it to the old man.

Benetsee puffed on the cigarette.

He blew out a long stream of smoke. He flipped the lit cigarette at the spruce tree behind him. The glowing butt landed on a branch and fire bloomed.

The fire ran around the tree, around and around, slowly wrapping the tree to the top.

The tree cracked and roared.

The fire went out at the top and it ran around and around the tree, on the same path, but down this time, till there was only the glowing end of the cigarette and then that flew back to Benetsee's hand.

He smoked.

He nodded to Du Pré and Madelaine.

He tossed the cigarette into the firepit by the sweat lodge and he was gone into the night.

Du Pré looked at the two Forest Service cops. One was trembling, the other standing stock still, eyes very wide.

Du Pré popped the clips out of their pistols and he checked the chambers and then he pressed out the bullets in the clips and he put the clips back in the empty guns and he went to the Forest Service cops and he stood there.

They were in a trance of terror.

"You are all right," said Du Pré. "You come on now it is time for you to go."

They looked at him and they looked at the guns he held out to them. They took them and then they looked at each other and they walked back up the little hill and got in their four-wheel-drive SUV and in a moment the engine started and then they were gone.

"Kidnapping," said Madelaine, "big wimps. They come here, arrest a medicine person. Kidnapping. Shit."

Du Pré laughed.

"I never see that before," he said. "Benetsee, him, he is always making fun, magic, never seen him do that."

"You have," said Madelaine, "just not so loud. He does, lots, just not so loud."

"That pretty loud," said Du Pré.

"You loud," said Benetsee. He was back again.

Du Pré trudged off to dig a jug of screwtop wine out of the trunk of his cruiser. He found one, wrapped in a towel, next to some plastic quarts of oil.

He carried it back down, hooking an empty jar from the porch as he went by.

The old man had two long drinks.

"Where is that Pelon?" said Madelaine.

"Canada," said Benetsee. "Belly River country."

Du Pré handed a jar of wine to Madelaine. She sipped it.

He rolled himself a smoke.

"Who is this bad person," said Du Pré, "kill old Maddy Collins?"

Benetsee looked off in the distance.

"You see him," he said. "You got to learn, see. Me, I am tired of seeing for you."

Du Pré nodded.

Benetsee was very old.

He had been old when Du Pré was a child, and that was nearly fifty years ago now.

Benetsee stood up. He yawned, turned, and stepped into the night.

Du Pré went to the firepit and held his hand over it.

He touched the ashes.

Cold and wet.

He laughed.

A giant bloom of fire grew into the dark, behind a long ridge that ran down from the flanks of the mountains.

It reached up and tongues licked the black sky and then it sank back down and there was only a red glow behind the ridge.

"God damn," said Du Pré.

"We maybe go soon," said Madelaine.

Du Pré nodded.

He put his hand on her shoulder and she got up and they walked back up the hill and around the cabin to the cruiser. They got in and Du Pré started the engine and backed the car out to the county road.

The front of the mountains was spackled with fires. Only one was large. It was above and around the place where Lou Dykstra had died.

Du Pré hit the steering wheel.

"Me, I want to ask him, the fire, what happen, Lou Dykstra," said Du Pré. "Old son of a bitch don't tell me nothing anyway."

Madelaine sighed, and she ran her fingers through Du Pré's hair.

"Old bastard," said Du Pré.

Madelaine coughed.

Du Pré drove on, the headlights found some mule deer on the road, eyes bloodred in the beams.

"That Lou Dykstra he is burned, gasoline. That fire is set. Some son of a bitch, leave a can hidden, it blows up," said Du Pré. "Maybe some of these other fires they are his."

Madelaine was looking out the window.

There were many deer in the pastures, driven down from the mountains by the fires.

A huge porcupine waddled across the road. Du Pré slowed down.

"Old son of a bitch," said Du Pré.

Madelaine patted his leg.

"Him not talk, you," she said, "him talk, me."

Du Pré looked at her.

"I know him, this man," said Madelaine.

Benetsee.

Damn.

"It is you this time?" said Du Pré.

Madelaine nodded.

"Benetsee talk, me," she said. "Him say I see this time."

Du Pré nodded.

"What do I do?" he said.

Madelaine shrugged.

"Don't say," she said.

"What he say to you?" said Du Pré.

"Not him," said Madelaine, "the Singers. They are singing a song. I don't know, words, but a couple, Benetsee he tell me what they are."

Du Pré slowed again: there was another porcupine on the road. The slow animals were getting away from the flames while they could.

Du Pré waited.

Madelaine was staring off into the distance.

He pulled over on a snowplow turnaround and stopped.

"Just this name, is all," said Madelaine.

Du Pré waited.

"Ash Child," said Madelaine.

Du Pré looked at her.

"That is what they sang," she said.

CHAPTER
18

Du Pré sat on the seat of the bulldozer, watching the fire crown out and run. He spat.

Hour ago I could have knocked down trees, cut a line. But they say no, it is too dangerous, the fire might catch you. Me, I cannot tell, trees are burning or not. I don't got a degree, fires. Been fighting them many years but I don't know anything.

Du Pré rolled a cigarette. He lit it.

"Put that out!" screamed a voice behind him.

Du Pré turned. A woman in Forest Service greens stood there, her face red.

"No smoking!" she yelled.

Du Pré looked at the raging blaze in front of him.

He looked at her.

"Go and talk, the fire there," he said. He had a long drag and he looked coolly at her.

She whipped out a ticket book and began scribbling.

Du Pré nodded. He stubbed the cigarette out and he waited.

"You got a driver's license?" she said, when she had walked up to Du Pré.

"Yah," said Du Pré.

She held out her hand.

Du Pré sat there, looking at the fire.

"Well?" she said.

"You writing a ticket?" said Du Pré.

"You're damn right," she said.

"Good," said Du Pré. "Me, I pay taxes, think if you write a ticket you maybe ought, write a good one, me, I get my tax money's worth."

He pulled the throttle back on the big diesel engine and he put the 'dozer in high gear and he clanked off toward a place where if he cut a line the fire might coil up and stop.

The big engine was very loud and he couldn't hear the woman yelling.

Du Pré crashed through a stand of young lodgepoles, headed for a rise near a coulee that held a little creek.

He dropped the gears down and gave the throttle a push to slow the engine a little and set the blade and began to push uphill, plowing up earth and trees. He looked over to his left. The fire was banging and bellowing. He had maybe ten minutes.

He went on up the slope to a rock spur, and then he wheeled the huge machine around. Going downhill he had more weight to use, so he shifted up and the blade knocked over big trees and the big steel treads walked right over the trunks.

Du Pré bashed his way down the hill.

There were several Forest Service people down there with the woman now, all waving their arms and shouting.

Du Pré got to the end of his run and he wheeled the machine around and he clanked back up the hill, bashing down more trees and brush and cutting the line wider.

The fire was getting close.

Du Pré hunched down and turned his hat toward the heat and kept on.

At the top of his run he turned around again, and he put the throttle way up and went to fourth gear and he roared down the mountain, the tonnage of steel crashing through the stand and not slowing at all.

The wall of heat was very hot and very near. Du Pré could feel the radiation on his right cheek.

A tree in front of him caught fire up high. Du Pré knocked it down and it fell into the flames.

The diesel roared and the timber splintered and cracked and Du Pré carved off the last slice and he was back down in the meadow where he had begun.

The Forest Service people stood there grimly.

Benny Klein's car was coming toward them, slowly, and the flashers suddenly went out.

Du Pré felt something burning on his neck. He tore off his shirt and shook out the coal that had fallen and stuck to the back of his collar.

He clanked past the Forest Service people and when he got near Benny's car he put the gears of the 'dozer in neutral and he set the throttle low.

Du Pré stepped down from the 'dozer.

Benny got out of his car. He was grinning.

"My, my," he said. "Why, the calls I been gettin'. You goddamn endangerin' son of a bitch! Will you look at those nitwits?"

The Forest Service people were marching over in a body.

"That's him!" said the woman who had been writing Du Pré the ticket.

"That's Gabriel Du Pré," said Benny, "I know it's him."

"Arrest him," said the woman. She began to recite the laws that Du Pré had broken.

Whocka whocka whocka whocka went a helicopter overhead.

Du Pré looked up at a TV camera, which was looking down at him.

Benny stepped away from them, hands on hips, and he looked at the fire.

It had raged up to the line Du Pré had cut and it was blowing and roaring but it had stopped.

"Good work," said Benny.

"They don't want nobody hurt," said Du Pré, "so do nothing you probably won't get hurt."

Whocka whocka whocka whocka.

"Channel Fifteen," said Benny, "got the whole darn thing on tape."

Du Pré looked up again.

A man was hanging out of the door, his right thumb up.

Du Pré held his arm up, thumb up, and he and Benny laughed.

The Forest Service people had seen the TV news helicopter. They were in a huddle.

"Six o'clock news," said Benny. "Brave Cat driver Gabe Du Pré cuts a fireline, stops part of the Wolf Mountains fire, and is then busted for doing it."

"Yah," said Du Pré, "crime, government, do something."

"Well," said Benny, "they do a lot, you know. Them Red Chinese ain't never landed in San Diego."

Du Pré laughed.

"I get to write tickets, folks who won't wear seat belts," said Benny. "Not that our law-abiding citizens would dream of not wearing seat belts. I never see a person isn't wearing one, myself."

Du Pré nodded.

"Drinkin' and drivin' is another," said Benny. "Why, if I see a citizen barreling down the road with a can, it's always pop."

The Forest Service people were moving toward them.

"Now?" said Benny.

Du Pré nodded.

Benny threw him against the car while mumbling a version of the *Miranda* warning not found in law. He handcuffed Du Pré and shoved him in the backseat.

The Forest Service people halted, horror-struck.

Whocka whocka whocka whocka went the helicopter with the TV camera.

Benny got in his cruiser, turned on the lights and the siren, and roared away.

Du Pré undid the handcuffs, which Benny hadn't locked.

He put them on the seat and he took out his pouch of tobacco and he rolled himself a smoke. He rolled down the window.

"Roll that goddamn thing back up," roared Benny. "We got 'em going now, don't fuck it up."

Du Pré rolled the window back up.

"I put the handcuffs back on, we get there," he said.

"Please," said Benny, "I have had more chickenshit calls from these turkeys than you can imagine, usually about somebody actually doin' something. We'd a probably done better they hadn't come."

Du Pré laughed.

There were two thousand firefighters in the Wolfs, and they were good, if they were allowed to do their jobs.

Du Pré bent down and he scanned the sky.

The helicopter wasn't there.

He looked at the ground to the left.

The shadow of the machine was there.

The TV crew was right overhead. They knew a story when they saw one.

Benny roared out on the bench road and he headed for Cooper.

Du Pré smoked.

"This is *fun*," said Benny.

"Yah," said Du Pré.

CHAPTER
19

The Toussaint Saloon was packed with people. It was exactly time for the Billings news channel to provide the state news of the day.

A beautiful, immaculately coiffed and chicly dressed young woman recited the day's main events.

"... and near the Wolf Mountains a man is arrested for fighting a fire," she said.

Cheers.

Whistles.

The ranch folk started chanting "Yea, Du Pré! Yea, Du Pré! Yea, Du Pré!"

"You ain't thinkin' of runnin' for my job, are ya?" said Benny.

Du Pré shuddered.

"Non," he said.

"Du Pré the Sheriff," said Madelaine. "Him, he don't arrest many people, that Du Pré."

"Neither do I," said Benny, "Better just to talk to 'em. Like that damn Justin kid. Little pain in the ass is back, ya know."

Du Pré looked at him.

"He is in, the Army," said Du Pré.

"No," said Benny, "I dunno what the story is. I know you took him down there, thought he enlisted. But he's been back. Kept out of sight a while. His mother went to get him, you know."

Du Pré nodded.

"Little shit," he said. He fingered the place on his head where Justin Wyman had hit him with the nail puller. There was a dent there.

"He didn't go back to school," said Benny. "Been out the Taylor ranch, workin' fencin' and such."

Du Pré nodded.

He shrugged.

"Him back?" said Madelaine.

"Yeah," said Benny, "he's been keepin' out of sight. I seen him couple of weeks ago, anyway."

A cheer went up from the crowd. A huge yellow 'dozer was crashing down a mountainside, trees going down like hay before the mower, and Du Pré could easily be seen, holding on to his hat.

Shot of Benny's car pulling in.

Shot of Forest Service people, standing smugly, watching Du Pré get down from the 'dozer.

Shot of the fire stopping at the line, thwarted. The flames roared and danced but they did not jump the line.

Shot of Du Pré up against the car, being handcuffed, and then shoved in.

"Why was this man being arrested?" said the TV reporter. "Apparently for fighting a fire. Forest Service personnel refuse to comment."

Shot of a silver-haired man in starched greens shoving through a throng of reporters.

"Is this the way to fight fires?" said the announcer.

"It's the way the goddamn government fights fires!" yelled a rancher.

There were no Forest Service people in the saloon. They knew better.

"Conflicts on the firelines," said the announcer. "The governor will speak, right after these messages."

Susan Klein killed the sound. Cutie-pies pushed useless things at all America.

"Governor loves this," she said, "just loves it."

She put a piece of paper in front of Du Pré.

"77," it said.

"That's the number of drinks people have bought you," said Susan. "I doubt you want 'em all at once."

Du Pré laughed.

He got up.

Madelaine looked at him.

"*Non,*" she said.

"I talk to him," said Du Pré.

Madelaine shook her head.

"Not now," she said. "You leave him alone now."

Du Pré looked at her.

"We have this deal," he said.

Madelaine shook her head.

"You tell him what to do is not a deal," she said. "He don't want, the Army maybe."

"Him don't want, Deer Lodge maybe," said Du Pré.

"Du Pré," said Madelaine, "I am thinking. I am thinking, Maddy Collins now, the fires. So maybe you just drink your seventy-seven drinks, don't fuck with things."

Du Pré's eyebrows shot up.

Madelaine put her lips close to his ear.

"What does 'Ash Child' mean?" she said.

Du Pré spread his hands.

"Me, I do not know either, but sometime, I know. It is mine this time. They speak, me, this time, Du Pré."

Madelaine kissed him.

"Dangerous," said Du Pré.

"Me, too," said Madelaine, "I am ver' dangerous."

She smiled.

Du Pré laughed.

"Children I know about," said Madelaine, "this riddle is for me, Du Pré."

Du Pré spread his hands.

Madelaine looked past him.

There was a man standing there, a tall man with a thick shock of blond hair and a tanned face. He was perhaps thirty-five and he was wearing a tan shirt with several pockets in it, all of which had stuff in them.

"Mr. Du Pré," he said, "I apologize for interrupting. I'm Frazier. Fire investigator. I'd like to talk to you about the fatal fire you witnessed. If now isn't convenient, I would like to set a time."

Du Pré looked at him, and then at Madelaine.

"Go on," she said, "you go talk now. Bastard who killed Lou Dykstra, him we want, *non?*"

Du Pré nodded. He made for the side door. Frazier followed him.

The air was cool outside. September, and day and night were about equal in length, and the air chilled rapidly when the sun left it, though it was still plenty light out.

Frazier lit a filter-tipped cigarette and waited while Du Pré rolled a smoke and then he held out his flaming lighter so Du Pré could light his.

"I was at the place where the fire blew up all day," said Frazier, "and I wanted to see what you might remember."

Du Pré thought.

"Popping, there was popping," he said. "Then the fire it blows up, very fast, I think I smell gasoline. Then some people come down, where Benny and I are, they are there, soot all over, and then Lou Dykstra walks down, the mountain, burned bad, his skin hanging from him."

Frazier nodded.

"It was set, it was arson," said Frazier. "Gasoline. A two-gallon plastic jug, like you put water in, and then several pint plastic bottles. Ordinary soft-drink bottles. He was setting small fires near the bottles and he would be away from the area before they burst and the gasoline went up. But something frightened him off. He left the two-gallon jug hidden under some brush. Lou Dykstra must have been standing next to it when it exploded. I'm amazed, seeing the splash the gasoline fire made, that he didn't die instantly. He must have covered his face and not breathed and rolled down the mountain. His clothes burned off him. It happened rapidly."

Du Pré slammed his fist into his palm.

"Set the fires," he said, "sometimes, people they set fires, get jobs fighting them. But they don't no more, Forest Service won't hire people local usually."

"I see from the news," said Frazier, "that it is better not to. You certainly set them up. You and the Sheriff."

Du Pré looked innocent.

Frazier laughed.

"I'm a consultant," he said, "I teach, actually. New Mexico. I study fire. Both historically, and its forensic behaviors."

Du Pré nodded.

"This is interesting," said Frazier. "I think that perhaps the only set fire was the one that killed Dykstra. The others, probably lightning. I wonder why someone would set a fire there?"

Du Pré shook his head.

"I have been carefully looking at the maps," said Frazier, "and I can't see anything. I have flown over the area. It's a poor place if you wished to set off a great blaze. Too many limiting factors."

Du Pré nodded.

"My card," said Frazier. "I'm staying in a campground, in my van. But I have a cell phone. I wondered if you might look at the maps and see if there is any reason at all why the fire would be set there."

Du Pré nodded.

CHAPTER
20

Du Pré walked through the black ashes. There were stakes with red surveyor's tape stuck in the earth, and yellow mason's line strung between them.

Near a blackened pile of charcoal, the remains of some branches piled near a big rock, he found a melted glob of blue plastic.

The jug. The firebug had been filling pop bottles with the jug on the rock. He had heard or seen something. He had hidden the jug and the bottles. Some of the bottles had been filled.

He had already started a fire.

Why would he start the fire before he was ready to leave?

Du Pré shook his head.

He looked up the hill. Blackened tree trunks still stood, and the ground was thick with ashes and charred pieces of trees. The fire had run up there.

The wind that day was from the southwest.

This was a dead forest, a place where pinebark beetles had girdled the cambium on thousands of lodgepole pines and they had died, their circulation cut. They had dried in the years, become better fuel.

Fire runs up mountains. It can run down them, too, if the wind is right.

This one ran up.

Du Pré sighed.

The ashes were thick and the mountainside steep and his boots would slip on the shadow of the fire.

He began to walk up the hill.

He stopped a hundred feet up and he looked around.

He tried to think what the forest had looked like before it burned.

Where would the deer trails be?

Deer always found the easiest way up and down mountains.

Du Pré looked at the ground and tried to pick his way on the easiest grades.

The going was hard, his feet slipping on the ashes, slick in their burnt layers.

Du Pré stopped. There was a tree trunk just ahead, black and burnt. It lay across another log.

He looked at it.

That is a body, he thought.

He went closer, and could see teeth, gleaming white out of black char.

Du Pré knelt by the charred corpse. The legs and arms had been shrunk by the heat and the body looked as if it were boxing. The hands were burnt away.

Blackened metal on the left wrist. Du Pré grabbed it.

A watch. The plastic face had melted but the metal band and works case were there.

Du Pré looked but he couldn't see anything else. Maybe a ring, but it would have fallen into the ashes.

Du Pré stood up.

He looked at the watch, a cheap one, Timex.

He went down the hill.

He switched on the two-way radio. The dispatcher in Cooper who hated him finally came on, sounding pissed at being distracted from her movie magazine.

"It is Du Pré," he said. "I need, talk to Benny."

"Why?" said the dispatcher.

Du Pré stayed silent.

"Well, be that way," she said. She switched off.

Du Pré cursed and he put the mike back in its cradle and started his cruiser.

The bitch at the Sheriff's office had been hating Du Pré since she knew he was alive.

He backed around and roared off down the steep winding road and when he came out on the bench road he turned toward Cooper. He had driven a mile when he stopped, hard, turned around, and headed back to Toussaint.

Susan Klein was sitting on her stool behind the bar, resting her legs. The mirror that had slashed her tendons when it fell on her in the earthquake had been heavy and she ached still and always would.

"Where is that Benny?" said Du Pré.

Susan shrugged.

"Me," said Du Pré, "me, I got, talk to him."

She looked at him.

"Oh," she said, "you already tried the bitch. Christ. Benny is so kindhearted he won't fire her. Lemme see what I can do." She went off to the back. She came back and she nodded.

"He's about a mile away and coming in a minute," she said. "Now, what is it? You, as my Irish grandmother would say, have a brow on you."

"There is a dead person, the fire that killed Dykstra," said Du Pré.

Susan put her hand to her mouth.

"Who?" she said.

Du Pré shook his head.

"My God," said Susan. "My God. You don't know who?"

"Who is missing?" said Du Pré.

"Couple of kids," said Susan. "Willie Pullen and Beth Sarkisian. They took off, everybody thought they eloped, went over to Idaho to get married and haven't got up the courage to call home yet."

Willie and Beth, Du Pré thought, the kids who came to Maddy Collins's to look around.

"Just the one?" said Susan.

Du Pré nodded.

I don't see the other one, but I see them magpies, ravens, down in the brush below. That is where the other one is. God damn.

"Willie he is looking for work maybe?" said Du Pré.

"You know how hard it is to find a job here, Du Pré," said Susan, "especially when you're only seventeen."

A car pulled in and stopped.

Du Pré nodded to Susan Klein and went out the door and found Benny getting out of his car.

"Got one, ver' bad," said Du Pré.

Benny looked pale. He hated violence and death and he had a weak stomach to go with his good heart.

"Need the coroner," said Benny.

Du Pré shook his head.

"This person is murdered, bad burned after," said Du Pré. "I think there is another one up there, too."

"Willie and Beth?" said Benny.

Du Pré pulled out the blackened twisted watch.

Benny looked at it.

"Oh, God," he said. "I hate havin' to bring news like this."

"This is his?" said Du Pré.

"I don't know," said Benny, "but I know."

Du Pré nodded.

"The state," said Du Pré, "they get us some help."

"What happened up there?" said Benny.

Du Pré shook his head.

"I go there now," he said. "You get them state people, come with them."

Benny nodded.

"This, they'll fly," he said. He switched on his radio.

Du Pré got in his cruiser and he drove down to Madelaine's. She was out in her yard watering the flower beds.

He got out of the car and he looked at her.

She shut the hose off and went into the house and came out wearing a light jacket and hat and leather lace-up boots.

She got in the car.

"It is those kids," she said. "Where are they."

"Where Dykstra is burned," said Du Pré.

Madelaine nodded.

"You come, get me," she said. "That is good."

"It is ugly," said Du Pré.

"Yes," said Madelaine.

"One is bad burnt," said Du Pré, "other maybe rotted some."

Madelaine nodded.

"You don't have, go there," said Du Pré.

"Yes," said Madelaine, "I do."

Du Pré started the cruiser.

He drove up toward the Wolf Mountains.

They didn't speak as he drove.

CHAPTER
21

Du Pré looked down through the grove of willows and small aspens that filled the little coulee. It had burned above the brush, and below it a little farther on, but this had not been touched.

"You maybe wait here," he said to Madelaine.

"You maybe fuck off," said Madelaine. "I see plenty bad things, my life."

"What is there I think is there," said Du Pré, "you have not seen it this bad. So why don't you maybe sit here, I yell to you."

Madelaine shook her head and began to walk down the deer path that cut through the patch of brush.

She gagged.

She coughed and choked.

Du Pré smelled it, too.

Nothing smell deader than a dead person, longtime dead, he thought.

Madelaine suddenly turned and ran back up the trail.

Du Pré looked past her.

A hugely bloated corpse lay in the brush on the downhill side. The blouse had been torn open by the ballooning abdomen. The belly hadn't burst yet. When it did the atrocious stink would enter any porous material near and it would take years to wash away.

Du Pré backed away.

One is in the fire maybe, it is two then they were shot.

Willie and Beth.

Seventeen, sixteen years old.

Out here setting fires, so Willie he can get a job fighting them.

Du Pré walked up the hill to Madelaine, who was leaning against a tree and vomiting.

He waited until her heaves stopped.

He touched her shoulder.

"Du Pré," she gasped, "I am sorry I am not so tough."

"Me either," said Du Pré. "We let people do this, their work do all of it. We go back now."

"It is them, yes?" said Madelaine.

"Yes," said Du Pré, "one of them, here, maybe it is somebody else. Two of them, one in girl's clothes, boy's watch on the other, it is them."

"Yah," said Madelaine, "we maybe go now."

Du Pré took her by the arm and he walked her gently back to the car. He got his flask from under the seat and poured some whiskey in a tin cup and gave it to her. She drank it like water.

She nodded.

Du Pré had some, too.

"Two dumb kids," she said.

"They came, Maddy Collins house," said Du Pré, "are looking in the windows I don't say nothing. They both sound real scared. But me, I don't think they are bad kids. They are out here setting fire though."

"People make a joke, that," said Madelaine. "They say, 'My

grandfather set fires, get a job fighting them,' and everybody laugh. But these kids they are dumb, actually do it."

"Yah," said Du Pré.

He rolled a smoke.

"They were not bad kids," said Madelaine.

Du Pré nodded. Not very good at doing bad things, either. Somebody else was. Shoot them both, and then they are gone before the people get here, fight the fire.

Du Pré looked around. He got out of the cruiser and he walked around the big trailhead circle.

He looked down from the built-up side.

Trails all over.

Dirt bikes, those four-wheel things, go anywhere.

The trails went off down the foothill, and into the trees on the slopes below.

Du Pré shook his head.

Shoot the kids, drive down there before the first pickup gets here, maybe got a truck down there, put the bike in it, drive home while they are all fighting the fire.

Benny and me don't see anybody coming *down.*

We are looking up at the smoke.

But it took a while for the smoke.

How long, a fire, next to a pop bottle, how long it burn before the pop bottle breaks?

Fire it is going the people they are here to fight it. They go up, try to cut a line, Dykstra he goes over by the rock, then it explodes.

How long that take?

Maybe couple of hours, day is still, fire is little and taking time to burn to the gasoline.

Frazier. I got to talk to Frazier.

Son of a bitch, maybe a long time. The killer, Willie, Beth, is long gone, smoke starts up.

Shit.

But somebody see him.

Why him kill them?

Du Pré shook his head and he walked back to the cruiser and he got in. Madelaine was touching up her makeup.

"I am sorry," she said.

"It is ver' bad," said Du Pré. "Come on we go, the saloon, there is nothing for us here."

Frazier he misses the body up on the hill, but he is looking where the fire starts.

Fire goes away, they are fighting it far off.

Nobody smells the girl, maybe smoke, wind is right not to.

When are they killed?

"Du Pré," said Madelaine, "what are you thinking?"

Du Pré shook his head.

"Me," he said, "this Beth, Willie, they are both shot I bet. But we do not know when. Maybe they are not shot just before the fire. Maybe they are shot, night before, two nights before. Maybe the fire it is set later."

Madelaine nodded.

"That guy, talk to you?" she said.

"Frazier," said Du Pré. "We go maybe talk to him."

Madelaine nodded. She held out the tin cup and Du Pré gave her more whiskey.

"Whew," she said, "let us go, Toussaint Saloon."

Du Pré backed around and drove down the road to the bench, and then when he got to the wider gravel road he accelerated.

They are killed at night.

Willie he shove Beth toward the brush, tries to save her, runs up the hill, easy target. But he does not.

Two killers?

Du Pré shook his head.

Now they got to go over that ground, fine sieves.

He turned and headed out toward the wide county road, and then he wheeled right and they could see little Toussaint out on the plain below.

110

"It is ver' bad," said Madelaine. "I get a ver' bad feeling there."

Du Pré nodded.

Place like that it has bad air.

The earth remembers, screams and blood.

He pulled up to the saloon and he stopped and they went in.

Susan Klein looked up.

"Jesus, Madelaine," she said, "what is wrong?"

"It is that Beth and Willie they are dead," said Madelaine. "It is ver' bad."

Susan Klein came around the bar and she hugged Madelaine and held her.

"Don' let the parents go there," said Madelaine, "there is nothing they would know there."

"Benny's waiting at the airfield for some state people," said Susan. "Tell you what, let me . . ."

"I will go," said Du Pré.

He walked out the door and across the road and toward the little airfield.

Benny was sitting on the hood of his car, looking to the southwest.

Du Pré took a few minutes to get there.

Benny looked at him.

"They girl is there, too," said Du Pré. "She did not burn."

Benny nodded.

He sighed and he got up.

"Could you go and get Father Van Den Heuvel?" said Benny.

"Yah," said Du Pré.

CHAPTER
22

The forensic team was large, fourteen men and women, and they had stretched lines across the places most likely to have evidence in them. Around the spot where the gasoline jug had exploded, killing Lou Dykstra, and around the charred body of Willie and the terribly rotted corpse of Beth.

Du Pré and Madelaine stood back out of the way. Frazier stood near them. They looked at the people in their moon suits, carefully probing the ashes, carefully photographing and measuring the dead.

"I never goddamn looked *up*," said Frazier. "I found what I came to find, and that was all I saw. If I were one of my graduate students, I'd suggest they consider another discipline. I am ashamed."

"Maybe," said Madelaine, "this save, one, two graduate students."

"Yup," said Frazier, "here I am, widely thought to be the best in my field, and look at this. I *know* what charred corpses look like. I've seen over eighty. I would have seen that one, if I had just looked up."

"Maybe not," said Madelaine.

"No," said Frazier, "maybe not."

He laughed, his face amused, with himself.

Du Pré nodded.

This Frazier he is all right.

Man laugh at himself he is foolish he is all right.

"You come, dinner," said Madelaine. "They won't let us look now anyway."

They left then and Frazier got in his old Jeep and Du Pré and Madelaine led the way to her house.

She found some spiced pork and black beans and rice and she put it in the oven to heat and she made a salad and got a loaf of her good bread from the pantry.

Frazier sat at the kitchen table, looking off somewhere.

Du Pré went to the telephone. He fished Pidgeon's number out of his wallet.

"This is Pidgeon," said the answering machine. "Leave a message."

Du Pré had started to speak to the tape when she picked up the phone.

"Yo, Du Pré," she said.

"Yes," said Du Pré, "this is strange now. You were not right."

"Of course not," said Pidgeon, "I'm merely right eventually. See, I made a guess. Didn't work out. How, you will tell me, because there is nothing you rednecks like better than an Eastern dude fucking up. So go ahead, rub it in."

"The dog is killed by this little shitbag I think is in Pine Hills, juvenile prison," said Du Pré. "He hates Susan Klein, she was his teacher. So he gets out, Pine Hills, is bringing dope back to Cooper and Toussaint, and so he kills Susan's old dog, burns down Maddy Collins's house."

"OK," said Pidgeon.

"Kid is out there while I am sleeping, I scare him, he whacks me the nail puller, runs," said Du Pré.

"OK," said Pidgeon.

"Two kids come earlier, I don't say nothing, they are snooping around not making trouble, so they get scared, leave," said Du Pré.

"OK," said Pidgeon.

"They are gone, people think they are, Idaho, gone there to get married. But they are not. Boy, he is setting fires, so he gets a job fighting them, she is with him, somebody kill them both."

"OK," said Pidgeon.

"So that is all I know," said Du Pré. "It was not the same person, like you said."

"OK," said Pidgeon.

"That all you got to say?" said Du Pré.

"No," said Pidgeon.

"So?" said Du Pré.

"Well," said Pidgeon, "you got a real psycho there for sure. Thing is, what you got to do now is go back and get all the *times* you can. Time for Maddy Collins, time for you at the house, the kids coming, you getting whacked."

"I find the kid, hit me."

"OK," said Pidgeon.

"It's in the times, eh?" said Du Pré.

"Usually is," said Pidgeon.

"How come you are not right?" said Du Pré.

"Look, dickhead," said Pidgeon, "you watch these dork TV shows where some tomato got tits out to there goes in a trance, sees the foul criminal in the act, and all. Well, what I do is ask what is going on and tell you what it looks like. From here."

"OK," said Du Pré.

"For instance," said Pidgeon, "what kinda weather we having here in good old Washington, D.C., right now?"

"OK," said Du Pré.

"Guesswork," said Pidgeon.

"It is raining," said Du Pré.

"No," said Pidgeon, "but it did earlier this afternoon."

"OK," said Du Pré.

"One thing I can tell you," said Pidgeon.

"Yah," said Du Pré.

"It's in the times," said Pidgeon. "Get pencil and paper and work out all of the times for everybody. Fires, murders, all of it. Last time the dead were seen. That stuff."

"OK," said Du Pré.

"You'd be surprised," said Pidgeon.

"Maybe," said Du Pré.

"Lemme know if I can help," said Pidgeon.

"Yah," said Du Pré. He hung up.

"She say what?" said Madelaine.

"Times, times everybody is killed, last seen, that."

"Timelines," said Frazier, coming back from wherever it was he had been.

"Yah," said Du Pré.

Frazier nodded.

"I'd like to do that," he said, "grunt work. Go back to the basics. Take notes. Do research."

"You are chewing chunks out, your ass," said Madelaine, "no need. So you fuck up."

Frazier laughed.

"Timelines," he said.

"So," said Du Pré, "I am maybe not going to work the fires now. So maybe I go and see Justin Wyman."

"*Non,*" said Madelaine.

"Eh?" said Du Pré.

Madelaine didn't look up from slicing the shallot she was putting in the salad.

"Not yet," said Madelaine.

"Why not goddamn yet," said Du Pré. "Little pissant beats in my skull, we make a deal, him go, the Army. I take him, Billings, to the recruiter."

Madelaine nodded.

"Not yet," she said.

"Bullshit not yet," said Du Pré. "Little prick is at the Taylor place, maybe he is one, kills Willie, Beth, burns them up."

Madelaine sighed. She put her hands on the counter. She took a deep breath.

"They did not speak to you they spoke to me," said Madelaine. "That Benetsee says, you, Madelaine, this is yours, eh?"

Du Pré threw up his hands.

"So," said Madelaine, "This time, my way."

Du Pré looked at Frazier, who was looking as far away as he possibly could.

"OK," said Du Pré.

Madelaine turned around.

"Do not fuck with me," she said, "don't get cute, do things, be that Du Pré he is always off, doing what he does. This time, my way, you don't screw things up this time."

"OK," said Du Pré.

"I, me," said Madelaine, "I got to sleep, maybe, outside tonight, I can hear."

"OK," said Du Pré.

"OK," said Madelaine.

She went back to the salad.

The stove buzzer sounded. Madelaine opened the door and stirred the beans and rice and closed the door. The spices smelled wonderful.

"My God," said Frazier. "What is that?"

"Bunch of stuff," said Madelaine. "You are going, find out the times?"

Frazier nodded.

"Take him with you," said Madelaine.

"OK," said Du Pré.

"Ten minutes we eat," said Madelaine.

"OK," said Du Pré.

"Take Frazier, your car," said Madelaine, "Get him a drink."

"OK," said Du Pré.

CHAPTER
23

Susan Klein was out in front of the Sheriff's office holding a woman who had fallen to her knees and who was screaming and screaming one thin note without pausing for breath.

Another woman had her head on her husband's shoulder.

The husband of the screaming woman was shaking his fist at the other couple.

Du Pré and Frazier watched from the cruiser, under the one lamp that burned on a pole near the street.

"Yer trash kid got mine killed!" said the man with the fist.

The other couple ignored him.

Benny came out of the office, with Father Van Den Heuvel in tow.

The woman on her knees was gasping now, and fairly quiet.

"OK," said Du Pré.

They got out of the car and they walked near but not close to the parents of Willie and Beth.

Father Van Den Heuvel knelt by Susan and the choking, gasping mother who had lost her daughter.

Susan and the big priest got the woman up off the ground and they walked her to a bench that sat in front of the office and they set her down gently on it. Susan sat next to her.

"Yer worthless goddamn kid!" screamed the man with the fist.

"Ralph," said Benny. "Shut up."

Ralph burst into tears, great heaving sobs. He turned away from Benny and he put his hands to his face.

"Mr. and Mrs. Pullen," said Benny, "I am so sorry."

The man looked up and nodded and went back to holding his wife. Their quiet grief was more terrible than the screams of the others.

Mr. Pullen finally led his wife toward a pickup parked across the street. It had one open door. An Australian shepherd stood in the bed.

He helped his wife in and shut the door and he came back across the street.

"When kin we have Willie," he said.

"I don't know," said Benny, "it's a criminal investigation."

Pullen nodded.

"Well," he said, "you'll let us know."

"Yes, sure I will," said Benny.

Pullen nodded at him and he walked across the street to the pickup.

Frazier went after him and asked a question.

Pullen thought for a moment and then he said something. He went to the open window of the pickup and spoke to his wife and he turned to Frazier and said something more.

Frazier nodded, and he turned and walked briskly back across the street.

"Sarkisians here are in a bad way," whispered Benny to Du Pré. "They never liked Willie and they set themselves above the Pullens. Pullens are good folks, had a lot of bad luck."

Du Pré nodded.

Another poor family that had lost its small ranch and was now working for wealthier neighbors.

"Sarkisian retired off the railroad," whispered Benny. "They ain't been around here too long."

Du Pré nodded. Newcomers around Toussaint were those whose forebears had arrived in the twentieth century.

"God," whispered Benny, "those poor kids."

Sarkisian had gone to the bench where his wife was. He put out his hand and touched her shoulder and she took his hand in hers.

Father Van Den Heuvel stepped away.

Du Pré went to him.

"They be all right?" he said.

"They will never be all right," said the big clumsy priest, "but I think the worst is over."

"They come, your church?" said Du Pré.

Van Den Heuvel shook his head.

"No," he said. "I don't know if they are at all religious."

Benny and Frazier joined them.

"Tuesday last," said Frazier, "was the last time the Pullens saw Willie. He left after supper, about six-thirty, drove off in the old car he had, and they never saw him again."

No old car by the fire, thought Du Pré.

"We need to find that car," said Benny.

"Yes," said Frazier.

"What kind of old car?" said Du Pré.

"An old Chevy," said Frazier, "1981 Nova. Gray with a lot of paint chipped on it. Broken windshield."

The dispatcher who hated Du Pré came out and waved at Benny and he walked over and went inside and then he came back out.

"I got to go," said Benny. "Got a bad accident out on the highway. Bill's out there. Listen, I dunno when I can get back. Somebody needs to see about that damn car."

"It is dark," said Du Pré.

"You're right," said Benny. He roared off, lights flashing, sirens screaming.

Frazier looked at Du Pré.

He looked at the Sarkisians.

Du Pré nodded.

Frazier went to Father Van Den Heuvel and the two of them talked for a moment and Van Den Heuvel nodded and he went to the couple on the bench. The priest knelt down and he asked a question.

The Sarkisians looked at each other and they both spoke at once and then they began to argue.

Father Van Den Heuvel listened patiently.

Finally the woman put her fingers to her husband's lips and she turned to the priest and said something. Father Van Den Heuvel got up and he came back to Du Pré and Frazier.

"Tuesday," he said, "she said she was going over to her friend Marsha's. They knew she was sneaking off to see Willie. But what do you do?"

Frazier looked at Du Pré.

"I figure nine days ago," he said. "Tuesday last would be two days ago."

Du Pré nodded.

Fire was five days ago, fire that killed Lou Dykstra.

They are up there dead four days maybe?

Four days, a long time.

"I am wrong," said Du Pré, "it is not that Willie setting the fires. They are up there, good place to screw maybe, they have been hiding out some, they find somebody already there."

Frazier nodded.

They run off not long after I speak, them, Du Pré thought.

He shook his head.

The car. The damn car. Somebody is up there, with the gasoline, the pop bottles, Willie and Beth come, they go up the mountain, they are killed. Killer comes back down, takes their car.

But how did he get there?

Du Pré shook his head.

Somebody got to have seen something.

God damn it.

"Du Pré," said Frazier softly, "the timeline is part of it, not that we know who-all should be on it."

Son of a *bitch*, Du Pré thought, me, I want to talk that little prick Justin Wyman.

"Justin Wyman," said Frazier.

Du Pré nodded.

"But Madelaine said for you to leave him alone," said Frazier.

Du Pré nodded.

"So what do we do?" said Frazier.

Du Pré looked off at the Wolf Mountains. There were still some glows from fires, high up, but the worst was over now.

Unless a hot wind that blew a hundred miles an hour came.

And it could.

Du Pré shook his head.

"What?" said Frazier.

"I think it is that Willie, setting fires, so he can fight them," said Du Pré.

"Pretty convoluted," said Frazier.

"We go talk, Madelaine," said Du Pré.

"Sure," said Frazier.

She is thinking something, someday she tell me, thought Du Pré.

Who is this bastard, kills Maddy, the kids?

Little shit Keifer maybe knows something.

Du Pré looked over at the jail.

The dispatcher was leaving and another woman was standing talking to her outside.

"Keifer," said Du Pré.

"Who is Keifer?" said Frazier.

Du Pré told him.

"He's in the jail over there?" said Frazier.

"Yah, I go talk to him," said Du Pré.

Frazier shook his head.

"Talk to Madelaine first," he said.

Du Pré looked at him.

"Shit," he said.

CHAPTER
24

Madelaine's car was gone when Du Pré and Frazier got back to Toussaint.

Du Pré drove to the Toussaint Saloon but the car was not there, either.

"Son of a bitch!" he yelled, pounding on the steering wheel.

"Where would she go?" said Frazier.

Du Pré put his hands in the air.

"She doesn't want us bothering people," said Frazier, "getting in her way."

Du Pré nodded.

"But we could go up to the site where the forensic team is," said Frazier. "Maybe they found something."

"They don't tell us probably," said Du Pré.

"Will if you ask right," said Frazier.

Du Pré roared off toward the bench road. They got to the

turnoff that went up to the trailhead and they could see lights on the mountain.

The team was working right through the night.

Du Pré slowed.

A deer bounced across the beams of the headlights.

Du Pré slowed a lot.

The deer ran back, ten feet in front of the cruiser.

"They always do that," said Frazier. "Had one come right rhough the windshield at me once."

"Yah," said Du Pré.

He pulled into the circular parking area at the trailhead. A pack of vans were pulled up, doors open, at the trail that led to the bodies and the evidence sites.

A cop in Highway Patrol uniform was standing near the trail.

A big red-faced cop.

McPhie.

Du Pré and Frazier got out and they walked to the trailhead.

"Stop right there," said McPhie. "The answer is no. Don't matter what the question is, the answer is no."

"Good evening," said Frazier.

"And to you, sir," said McPhie. "But the answer is still no."

"McPhie," said Du Pré, "this is Frazier."

"Charley Frazier the fire historian?" said McPhie.

Frazier nodded.

"Well," said McPhie, "the answer is still no."

"You don't like it here," said Du Pré.

"They could get a goddamn wooden Indian to do what I am doing," said McPhie, "Christ, the asswipe who is my boss sends me over here, says do what they need, they need a wooden Indian. They're all up there with tweezers and Baggies and me, I am down talking to an expert and a halfbreed outlaw."

"They find anything?" said Frazier.

"May well have," said McPhie. "Don't bother to burden me overmuch with information, though."

Du Pré looked up the hill.

"We go up there?" he said.

"The answer is no," said McPhie.

"McPhie," said Du Pré, "this is bullshit."

"True, laddie," said McPhie. "So much of life is, you know. But I have my orders, from the asswipe I work under, and so the answer is no."

"The car," said Frazier.

Du Pré nodded.

"A car?" said McPhie. "You are looking for a car. I myself have looked for many cars in my time, and even found some of them."

"These two kids, driving an old Chevy Nova," said Du Pré.

McPhie looked up the hill.

"Two of 'em," he said.

Du Pré looked at him.

"Long way from anywhere here. A car is missing, got two dead people, then it took two live ones, get the car gone."

Du Pré nodded.

"Yes," he said.

"There," said McPhie, "I feel so *useful*."

Footsteps.

A pair of technicians came down the trail, lugging an aluminum trunk.

"So," said McPhie, "you wish to find this car."

Du Pré nodded.

McPhie looked up at the stars.

"Make me an offer," he said.

Frazier looked at Du Pré.

"Two bits," said Du Pré.

"Sold," said McPhie, looking at the technicians working at something in a van. "My asswipe superior may go fuck himself. Two bits is a better offer. Now, what do we *know*?"

"Kids here take off, are hiding out," said Du Pré. "Don't know why they came up here or who kills them. But they are in the old Chevy."

McPhie nodded.

"Last seen nine days ago," said Frazier, "about six, six-thirty P.M."

McPhie nodded.

"Don't know yet how long they were dead?" he said.

Du Pré shook his head.

McPhie rubbed his nose. He walked over to the technicians in the van and he spoke for a moment.

He came back.

"The girl was killed eight or nine days ago," said McPhie. "They found maggots in her that take that long to get so big. And they were that big. So, it seems that they must have been killed the very evening that they were last seen."

Du Pré walked away, looking up at the mountains, while Frazier and McPhie talked in low tones.

Shit, Du Pré thought, they were meeting someone here.

Son of a bitch.

They are maybe running away, so they need money.

Meet somebody and get money.

What do they have that is worth money?

Something they have.

Something they know.

Du Pré slapped his forehead.

Blackmail.

They knew something.

They knew something very bad about somebody.

Poor dumb kids, they think that whoever it is kill Maddy won't kill them, too.

Has to be it.

He walked back to Frazier and McPhie.

They were still talking.

"Blackmail," said McPhie. "Nothing else fits. They were young kids, no money, nothing their families had that was worth a lot. That leaves something that they knew."

Du Pré and Frazier nodded.

McPhie looked up at the stars.

"I have a daughter," he said, "fine bonny lass, and married now with two babies, to a young feller I expect will have to do. He drinks California wines and talks about 'em too much. But she likes him OK."

Du Pré rolled a smoke.

"Now, when she was a young and beautiful wench and trying to send her dear old dad to the bughouse, she had a friend who was close enough to be a fucking Siamese twin. And those two had no secrets. They were on the telephone to each other about thirty-one hours a day, and they both kept *diaries*."

Du Pré looked at Frazier.

"Soooooo," said McPhie, "I was you I'd find that friend."

Du Pré nodded.

The technicians who had been in the van shut the doors and trudged past, not even looking up.

"So what is Benny doing?" said McPhie.

"Accident, the highway," said Du Pré.

McPhie nodded.

"Passed it coming in," he said. "A bad one."

Frazier looked around the trailhead.

"This," he said, "is a most interesting case."

McPhie nodded.

"We say that," he said, "when we don't know fuck-all about anything."

Frazier laughed.

There was a sibilant drone up the hill.

"God alone knows what gadget that is," said McPhie.

"Come on," said Du Pré, "I know where Madelaine is."

Frazier went with him.

McPhie pissed on the gravel.

CHAPTER
25

Du Pré dropped Frazier off at his motel in Cooper. The town was dark and dead, and only one or two lights shone in windows of houses.

"I'll drive over in the morning," said Frazier. He walked away and Du Pré drove off.

She don't tell me where she is going, to hell with her, Du Pré thought, these are bad people and I will not wait to see, she is all right.

He cruised the back road by the Taylor place where Justin Wyman was supposed to be working.

He drove in, lights off, and he could see the little ranch and the outbuildings, and Madelaine's car wasn't there.

Just three old pickup trucks and a larger four-ton grain truck.

The greenish light from a mercury-vapor lamp threw all the objects in its reach into sharp relief.

A dog began to bark.

Du Pré backed and turned and he drove on.

Benetsee, maybe she is there, sweating.

Du Pré drove on the bench road, slowing when he came to the top of a hill. Deer would run just out of sight on the other side and freeze when headlamps plunged down and caught them.

He turned into the driveway that led up to the old cabin. The cruiser wallowed in the ruts. The headlamp beams jumped and danced and Du Pré saw the rear end of Madelaine's Subaru, parked off the track.

He relaxed.

Now I get my stupid Métis ass chewed but me, I don't give a shit. Damn woman go off like that.

Du Pré laughed.

Madelaine do what she want, sometimes I like it, mostly I like it, piss me off when I don't like it and am scared.

Du Pré parked next to the little rice rocket and stopped the engine and he got out and he could hear the drumming.

They were singing down in the sweat lodge.

Healing song.

Du Pré sat on the back porch, listening to the chanting and singing from the sweat lodge.

Something moved behind him and he grabbed his nine-millimeter and turned.

Pelon stood there, holding a big cup of something that steamed.

"Shoot me, please shoot me," said Pelon. "I can't stand no more a that old bastard."

Du Pré laughed. Benetsee's apprentice sat down and sipped his tea.

"Bad times bad hearts," said Pelon. "They are trying to heal those bad hearts."

Du Pré nodded. Pray for your enemies: how sad life would be with no one to fight.

He shook his head.

"Old song," said Pelon, "old bad time reaches down the years and makes a new bad time."

Du Pré looked at him.

"That's all that I know," said Pelon. "You know how that old son of a bitch talks in riddles."

Something pale moved swiftly across the little meadow and disappeared.

Madelaine, naked, running from the sweat lodge to the creek to cool off.

Du Pré got up and he walked down the hill.

When he got to the pool Madelaine was out on the grass toweling herself.

She stood on the towel and began to put on her clothes.

Benetsee walked by, small and gnarled, and slowly.

"Great tits," said the medicine man, and he jumped into the pool.

Du Pré laughed.

Once I come here, they are in the sweat lodge, Pelon and Benetsee, they are singing a new sacred song.

"We all live in a yellow submarine . . ."

Du Pré looked at Madelaine, who hadn't said anything yet.

"You are pissed, me?" he said.

"*Non,*" said Madelaine, her voice a hoarse cracked croak, "I sing too damn hard."

Madelaine put her hand on Du Pré for balance while she pulled on a Creek moccasin that had the ties in back of the heel.

She put on the other and she walked to the stump near the creek and she sat and tied the thongs tightly.

Du Pré rubbed her shoulder. She put her hand on his.

"Terrible sad," she said, "it was very sad in there tonight. Lot of pain, lot of horror, longtime gone."

Du Pré waited.

"What we do now?" he said.

"Go get some sleep," she said. "Tomorrow I got people, see."

They walked up the path and around the cabin to their cars.

Pelon was gone and Benetsee had never come back out of the pool.

Du Pré drove off and Madelaine followed him.

They parked in front of her house and went on in.

Madelaine's eyes were deep with thought, and Du Pré made her tea. He put it in front of her and had to gently touch her before she noticed it. She clasped his hand.

He sat down and rolled a smoke and he lit it and passed it to her. She took the one long drag that she liked and handed it back.

"Hard stuff this," she said.

Du Pré nodded.

"Yah," he said, "ver' hard. It is hard, hear those voices, know that stuff and not know it, too."

"Benetsee him help but not too much," she said. "I never had a sweat like that, my life."

"Him carry that all the time," said Du Pré.

Madelaine shook her head, staring at her teacup.

"Ha," she said, smiling, "him start this he is twelve feet tall now he is some worn down."

They laughed and laughed. It wasn't that funny but they needed to.

"What we do now?" said Du Pré.

Madelaine looked at him.

"You, Frazier," she said, "find out, where everybody is. There is someone, can't see them, someone we don't know, it is that person who is so bad."

Du Pré nodded.

"Don't you talk, that Justin Wyman yet," she said, "that Keifer either. Me, I talk, them."

"OK," said Du Pré. "That Keifer is a piece of shit. He will not help you."

"He not help *you*," said Madelaine. "I am not you."

Du Pré lifted his eyebrows and spread his hands.

"OK," he said.

Madelaine reached across the table.

"I am not biting you," she said, "but it is important you don't talk, these people."

Du Pré looked at her.

"I don' know *why*," said Madelaine. "That is what they said. So you know 'bout that."

Du Pré nodded.

They talk, me, I listen, he thought.

"That Frazier," said Madelaine, laughing, "they say funny things about him. Say he spend much time not listening to them. You know, those people don't want, hear that stuff."

Du Pré nodded.

"I don't want, hear that stuff," he said. "I got to after that damn coyote is digging my backyard, where the box is tells me Catfoot kills Bart's brother. I don't want to listen you yet."

"Got to though," said Madelaine.

"That old bastard Benetsee," said Du Pré, "always joking. Always making fun of me, telling me his damn riddles I need, know something."

"Du Pré," said Madelaine, "have some whiskey."

Du Pré nodded and got up and went to the cupboard and got down a bottle of bourbon and he made himself a stiff ditch and drank it and he made another.

He sat down again.

"So maybe," he said, "it is all right you do more of this, I tend that bar, Toussaint."

Madelaine laughed and laughed.

"You are some jealous, me!" she said. "Du Pré' is being ver' foolish. You are pissed, old ones don't want, talk to you this time?"

"Non," said Du Pré, "I am worried, afraid for you."

"I be all right at the end," said Madelaine. "The old people they say that, too."

CHAPTER
26

"Alone," said Madelaine, "you go off, look for things, me, I stay at home, wondering, Du Pré is maybe dead out there, got a bullet, his head. You hunt, alone. You go to sleep, alone."

"I sleep with you," said Du Pré.

"Now when you *sleep*," said Madelaine, "me, I cannot be in your sleeping."

Du Pré nodded. Little death, practice for the big one.

"OK," he said.

"So," said Madelaine.

Du Pré looked off somewhere.

Madelaine sighed.

"It is hard for you," she said, "longtime gone, women, stay in the camp, the teepees, with the children, men, they are out many miles, watching for enemies, keep them away."

Du Pré nodded.

When we got Indian teepees, Métis carts.

"OK," said Du Pré, "me, Frazier, we help. If you want. But we don't get in your way."

"Good," said Madelaine.

Du Pré thought of Benetsee and his flames, the terrified Forest Service cops, the magic.

"Benetsee help you," said Du Pré. "He don't I maybe kill him."

Madelaine laughed.

"Du Pré," she said, "him know it drive you crazy, he will use it, drive you crazy."

Du Pré sighed.

"So," said Madelaine, "I got a couple questions. I buy this gun but maybe I do not know everything about it."

"Eh?" said Du Pré.

"They sell guns, women," said Madelaine. "We vote, too."

"What gun?" said Du Pré.

Madelaine fished a big black automatic pistol out of her beaded purse. She pulled back the slide. She popped out the clip. She gave the gun to Du Pré.

He held it. It was astonishingly light. He looked at the stamps on the slide.

"Who makes this?" he said.

"It is a Glock," said Madelaine.

"Glock?" said Du Pré. "It is plastic?"

"I shoot it," said Madelaine, "real slugs come out, the end there."

"Good," said Du Pré.

"So you don't know this gun?" said Madelaine.

Du Pré shook his head.

"OK," said Madelaine. She took it back and fiddled with it and it came apart and she laid the pieces on the table.

"Thing you want," said Du Pré, "you put it back together there you don't got pieces left over."

Madelaine nodded.

She put the Glock back together.

"Come on," she said. They went out in back of the house.

There was a piece of paper stuck on the side of an old cotton-wood stump.

Madelaine aimed and she fired.

The paper was untouched.

"I am doing something wrong," said Madelaine.

"You are not hitting, the paper," said Du Pré.

Madelaine looked at him for a long time.

She handed him the gun.

Du Pré fired six times.

The paper had six holes in it, no more than two inches apart.

Madelaine nodded.

"OK," she said. "What are you doing there."

"You are aiming," said Du Pré, "but you got to just shoot. Look at the paper. I get another one." He went into the house and he found a pad of stick-on notes and came back out with them. He put a fresh yellow piece over the one he had shot.

Madelaine frowned at the target.

"Look at the paper," said Du Pré. "Don't bother about the gun now."

Madelaine put her finger outside the guard and she pushed the gun forward a few times.

"That is good," said Du Pré. "Like a snake striking, you coil and stretch, there, fire when you are snapping your mouth shut."

Madelaine nodded.

She sighed and closed her eyes.

She coiled and stretched just a little, and each time she fired.

Du Pré crossed his arms and waited.

Eight.

The slide stood open. The gun was empty.

They went to the paper.

It had seven holes in it.

"I know which one I miss," said Madelaine. "I lose a beat."

"Yah," said Du Pré, "it is someone they are dead, though, this."

"It is low, a kneecap maybe," said Madelaine. "Me, I do not want to kill a person."

Du Pré nodded.

Madelaine filled the clip and racked a round into the chamber. She fired nine times.

"Holds more," said Du Pré.

"So what?" said Madelaine.

There were six new holes in the paper.

"Damn," said Madelaine.

"Don't do this too much," said Du Pré.

"Eh?"

"Shoot some, go away a while, shoot too much you get mad with yourself, you miss more and more you start thinking too much."

"Like you," said Madelaine.

"Yah," said Du Pré.

Someone cleared a throat behind them.

They turned and saw Frazier.

"I come in peace," he said.

Madelaine grinned.

"Yah," she said, "maybe you know something. Thing is, what did you have to do to know it?"

Frazier spread his hands wide.

"I've spoken with both sets of parents," he said, "and know a little more."

"OK," said Madelaine.

Frazier walked to the paper stuck on the stump. He whistled.

"I can't hit the *earth* with a pistol," he said, "I once tried to shoot a can. Immortal can. I used a hundred and twenty-two shells. The can was good as new. It's at home on my mantel. I sold the pistol."

"What you want the pistol for?" said Madelaine.

"Snakes," said Frazier.

"So use that ratshot," said Madelaine.

Frazier shook his head.

"I don't think it would help," he said.

They went into the house and Frazier and Du Pré sat at the table. Madelaine brought a section of newspaper and a cleaning kit and she took her Glock apart and cleaned it carefully. Du Pré made coffee.

"Beth's parents think that the kids were buying drugs some-place," said Frazier, "they didn't know where. Beth's eyes were too bright and she was confused from time to time."

Du Pré and Madelaine nodded.

"I guess drugs are a problem even here," said Frazier.

Madelaine nodded.

"Bad," she said, "ver' bad."

"Willie's parents didn't know what he was up to," said Frazier. "They didn't talk, I suspect because talking isn't something that they do well. So there they were, in silence. But Willie was a hard worker, did well in school, and he and Beth had plans, even though her parents didn't like Willie or his people."

"Old story," said Madelaine. "Did they ever find drugs?"

"No," said Frazier.

"They looked," said Madelaine.

"Beth's people did," said Frazier. "Searched her room."

Madelaine nodded.

"Marsha," said Madelaine, "that is Beth's friend's name, yes?"

Du Pré nodded.

"Marsha Leppert," said Frazier.

"I talk to her," said Madelaine.

Frazier nodded.

"She's in a drug rehab program in Minnesota," said Frazier.

"I know where Minnesota is," said Madelaine.

Du Pré looked at her.

"I got to pack," said Madelaine.

CHAPTER 27

"So we are coming day after tomorrow," said Maria. "Ben is done editing."

My daughter, movie star, thought Du Pré. Jesus, that Lewis and Clark movie was more trouble than the real ones had, walking from St. Louis, the Pacific, back home.

"Good," said Du Pré. He was standing at the bar in the Toussaint Saloon. A young mother with two squalling brats had just come in, in hopes of something for her nerves.

"Let me talk, Madelaine," said Maria.

"She is gone, Minnesota," said Du Pré. "She is looking for this person kill poor Maddy Collins."

"Oh," said Maria.

"Benetsee tell her to," said Du Pré.

"Oh," said Maria.

"Maybe you help," said Du Pré.

"I tell Madelaine you think she need, my help," said Maria, laughing.

"Shit," said Du Pré.

My women are always smarter.

"I pray, your Ben," said Du Pré.

"Too late," said Maria.

"OK," said Du Pré.

"But I help her anyway just don't tell her, you said that," said Maria.

"Ah," said Du Pré, "my life pass before my eyes, then it rewind."

"Love you, Papa," said Maria.

Du Pré shut the telephone off.

"Bobby," said the young mother, *"I am gonna stuff you in the toolbox!"*

Little Bobby looked up at Du Pré, his face curious.

Du Pré bent far over.

"You be good, I help her," he growled.

Bobby nodded, once.

"Be quiet, Sara," he said to his tiny sister. She shut up at once.

Du Pré went out and he got in his cruiser. He rolled a smoke and lit it and started the engine. He backed out and turned around and drove off, not much caring where.

Dry. Damn, it was dry. So dry the sun shining through a piece of broken glass could start a fire.

Du Pré drove up on the bench road that snaked along the foothills of the Wolf Mountains. The prairie lay huge to the south, the horizon purple and smudged.

Du Pré pulled off on a snowplow turnaround and he looked down on the land and the little town of Toussaint, small ramshackle buildings, as most towns were here. Impermanent, soon to be taken by the wind.

It was hot and the sun gathered heat in the car, metal hot to the touch, glass holding in stale air.

Du Pré got out. He walked around the front of the cruiser and got his binoculars from the glove box. They were old ones, Zeisses; Catfoot had brought them back from Europe when the Second World War ended. The leather case had a furrow, a crease, where a bullet had scored it.

"Him a sniper," said Catfoot, looking at the case one day, "kill our lieutenant, kill a couple guys stick their heads up too long. So I go out, dawn, find a good place, wait, look around, see this sheet of metal next, busted-down wall. Ah, I say, big enough, man hide there. I put my helmet, a stick, poke it up a little, wait, I see him look out, the shadow, stick out his rifle. But I am quicker, shoot him between the eyes. German officer, too, captain, he is sniping I don't know why."

Catfoot had also brought back an MP-40, a Schmiesser machine pistol, fired six hundred and forty rounds a minute.

It was in a rawhide case in the attic of Du Pré's old house, where Raymond and Jacqueline and their huge brood of children now lived.

Worked good, too.

Maddy Collins. Why someone kill Maddy Collins?

Kill her with a hatchet.

Maybe this all starts there.

Me, I cannot bother Nancy Wyman, Justin.

Madelaine don't say leave Maddy alone.

Du Pré got back in the cruiser and drove down the next road to the flat and wound around a back road to Maddy's place.

Blackened ruins.

The outbuildings still stood. A collapsing garage, built in the days when automobiles were the same size and shape as spring wagons. An old outhouse, unused, the door crooked and rotting. A shed, with galvanized metal roofing, a piece pried up by the winds. An old car on blocks. Still had the windshield but the door glass was gone.

That little shit Davy Keifer, mean as a weasel and dumb as dirt. Burns the place, puts Susan Klein's poor old dog in it. What a piece of shit he is.

Why all this, Maddy Collins?

Old lady some crazy live out here alone nobody hardly knows her.

Got to be some reason.

Du Pré walked around back of the old garage.

Skunk tracks, and the skunk had grubbed up some earth near one corner. Probably smelled a nice fat beetle grub.

Justin Wyman whack me here.

Davy Keifer burns it down.

Beth and Willie are here scaring themselves.

Poor old Maddy Collins.

Du Pré heard an automobile. It stopped.

He walked back around the garage.

Frazier got out of his van and waved to Du Pré.

"I thought you might be here," he said.

Du Pré waited.

Frazier ambled over.

"Well," he said, "I did what I should have done a long time ago. Went to the newspaper in Cooper."

County paper, came out once or twice a month.

"It isn't what you'd call a modern operation," said Frazier, "but I dug through the files. Real files. Dust made me sneeze. Then I went to the courthouse . . ."

Du Pré nodded. He looked up at the Wolf Mountains, blue in the heat haze.

"Nancy Wyman," said Frazier, "sure has a lot of fires in her past. Her husband died in one. Accident. Car rolled and caught fire."

Du Pré nodded.

"He drink a lot," said Du Pré.

"Sure," said Frazier, "so everybody figures he got drunk and rolled his pickup. Had to be an inquest anyway. Had to be an autopsy. State did it, no facilities here."

Du Pré looked at him.

"Nancy Wyman has lost two patients," said Frazier, "both heavy smokers, both set fire to the bedclothes, both died of smoke inhalation."

Du Pré nodded.

"Now," said Frazier, "Thing is that folks do die, everybody gets to, no exceptions, but, damn it, so many people around Nancy Wyman die of fire. Somebody oughta die of something else, you ask me."

Du Pré nodded.

"Madelaine say we leave her alone," said Du Pré.

"Oh, yes," said Frazier, "I get that, but what I thought I might do is ask about the autopsy of Nancy's husband, Justin's father. I would dearly love to know what they found. Whether they ran a screen on the man's blood. It was sixteen years ago. I would think they would have."

Du Pré looked at Frazier.

"Me, I have never seen her," he said, "I see most everybody here but her I never see."

Frazier nodded.

"Home health care," he said, "so she can't have much education. Low pay, long hours . . ."

Du Pré yawned.

"Madelaine be back soon," he said.

Frazier nodded.

"I sent an inquiry," he said, "asked them to fax me back."

Fax machines, Du Pré thought, maybe they are a good thing.

"It is her," said Du Pré.

"I'd bet it is," said Frazier.

Du Pré looked up at the mountains again.

"Me," he said, "I go maybe, ask old somebody, who Nancy Wyman is before she gets married."

"Yeah," said Frazier.

They walked to their rigs.

CHAPTER 28

"Madelaine called for you," said Susan Klein. She was sitting on her padded highbacked stool behind the bar, and rubbing her legs.

Du Pré nodded.

"She's on her way back," said Susan. "She was about a hundred miles west of Sioux Falls."

Du Pré nodded. Going north of the Black Hills, across Wyoming, past the Devil's Tower.

So she would be back maybe lunchtime tomorrow, if a Highway Patrol didn't stop her.

Or the pistons on the Subaru maybe went out the top of the block.

"And she said to remember not to bother those people," said Susan. She got up and went down the bar to the popgun, filled a glass with ice and put Coke in it and a lemon wedge.

"You want a drink?" she said.

Du Pré shook his head.

He got up and went out and drove off toward the Wymans' place. Justin's old truck was there and a light was on.

Old Mrs. Pritchett was where Nancy Wyman worked.

Buster and Billie Pritchett. Buster dead now twenty years maybe, cancer. Billie very old.

But they were tall and white-haired and sunbrown and they worked very hard on their little ranch. Billie was so stubborn that when she cut a finger off putting wood through a table saw she found it and blew off the sawdust and put it and some snow in a coffee can and stuck her wound in a bag of snow and drove one-handed to the clinic and demanded that the finger be put back on. When they couldn't do that she started to go out the door to drive to Billings.

Would have, too, but the doctor had already called the High-way Patrol, and one of the officers drove her there, lights and siren on.

Billie passed out from shock and age.

She was eighty-three.

Ten years ago maybe?

Ver' old lady now.

She would not like living so long.

Du Pré couldn't remember whether Billie had gotten her finger sewn back on.

She wouldn't leave her place, either.

Buster was out in the county cemetery and Billie would join him one day.

Me, I should have gone to see her. I like them both. I go a couple times after Buster dies and then I don't see Billie and so I don't go and I forget her.

Du Pré tried to think of the best place to get near the ranch.

Bench road to the Forest Service road up in the trees and then along the front of the Wolf Mountains until he was above the ranch, down the foothills, get in close.

Du Pré fished a burnt cork out of the box on the transom. He striped it down his cheek and looked in the rearview mirror.

Not burnt enough.

Du Pré put the cork back and drove on. He got to the Forest Service road and went up it; the fires had spared this stand of trees. The flames had cut higher on the flanks of the mountain.

He found a place to pull off. He burnt the cork with his cigarette lighter and waited for it to cool, then smeared his face with it. There was a coal still glowing and Du Pré felt it sear a small place on his skin.

He looked in the mirror.

His eyes were bright white, the pupils and irises black.

The light was still good, but it was three or four miles to the place on the mountain he wanted to look down on the Pritchett place from. There would still probably be one hand there, doing a ranch's constant work, even if the last beeves had been sold long ago.

Du Pré got some soft-soled Israeli desert boots from the trunk of the car. He put his nine-millimeter in a clip holster and stuck it on the back of his belt. Some whiskey and the binoculars went into a little pack.

The car was pretty well hidden, down at the end of a feeder track.

Du Pré put his hat on the backseat of the cruiser and he trotted off on a game trail that went fairly level across the flank of the mountain. It went down and he stepped over a tiny creek, scrambled up a low cutbank, and went on.

An hour later he was moving through the alders at a larger creek, Deer Creek, like a thousand other creeks in Montana. It was wide enough so he looked for a way over, but he couldn't find a place to cross dry-shod until he went downhill to another game trail that ended at a log somebody had set over the creek, compressed now where it had cut a cleft in the limestone of the mountain's bones. Whoever had done it had nicely leveled the top of the log. A good horse could have been led across it, a very good horse.

Du Pré trotted on. He stopped a couple of times to smoke and to rest.

Coming back in the dark would be pretty easy, once he set himself the right height on the mountain. A lot of elk came through here, and they were good engineers.

Du Pré came out on a grass slope, an old burn that had never gotten trees back on it. He could see the Pritchett place a mile or so away. He got out the binoculars and scanned the buildings. No one was moving around. There was a big old car and a new van, blue with black windows.

He trotted across the slope and back into the trees. When he thought he was directly above the ranch he moved down the slope, cursing the soft-soled boots which slipped on the loosened soil and rocks.

He kept to the trees, which came down fairly close to the ranch buildings. The Pritchetts had come into the country in the 1880s and had a good water right on a creek, and they had built a pond and planted cottonwoods to shade the house in summer. It was a low house, long, with shed-roofed additions. The original log cabin was off to the east, near the creek. The main house was two stories in the center though the second story was just the high-peaked roof with dormers in it.

Du Pré saw some movement and he dashed across to a better place to see what it was.

A tall handsome woman, slim and strong-looking, wearing a nurse's uniform, was pushing someone in a wheelchair over the bumpy ground toward the van. They got there and the woman opened the doors in the side and fiddled out a platform, hy-draulic. She got it down to the ground and pushed the wheel-chair on to it, fiddled with the controls again, and lifted Billie Pritchett up and into the van and shut the doors.

Billie was slumped and ancient, swathed even though the day was warm, and she had on a bright red hooded sweatshirt.

The woman in the nurse's uniform must be Nancy Wyman, Du Pré thought. Looks young for woman old enough to be Justin's mother.

Nancy Wyman got into the van and she backed it and turned

and drove down the ranch road toward the county road. Du Pré put the glasses on the van. When they got to the county road the van went to the right.

West.

So they were going to Cooper.

Du Pré looked around carefully with his eyes and then the binoculars.

No one seemed to be moving.

There was the big old car and that was it parked near the house.

A door *scrawk*ed as the night wind came up.

It was getting dark.

Du Pré smoked a carefully shielded cigarette.

Wait here a while, then I go on down there and look around.

He looked at the house. There was a single light burning in it.

Du Pré went into a hunter's trance, awake but barely breathing, waiting, waiting.

Catfoot he hunts snipers in the war, it is like hunting coyotes he says, find a good place and wait, then the coyote comes, sniper moves.

Du Pré heard the night sounds. A rabbit screamed in an owl's grip. Deer passing snorted when they scented him. The fiddlebow sound of one pine leaning upon another when the wind coughed.

The ranch house and the outbuildings stood dark and silent. The door creaked.

Headlights reached down the county road.

They slowed and turned into the crossbar.

Du Pré snapped awake.

CHAPTER
29

Du Pré closed his eyes so that his night vision would not be spoiled by the bright lights. It was that last quarter of the pupil opening that took so long.

He listened to the engine grind.

The van was quiet.

A truck, then, and not very new.

Justin, probably.

The truck engine ground up to the house and stopped and Du Pré heard a door open and shut, hard and metallic.

He opened his eyes.

Movement, by the equipment shed across the driveyard. A door slid open, the rollers *whack*ing a little.

Du Pré closed his eyes again.

Probably a light in there, come on now.

He waited.

He opened his right eye, barely, and he could see light pouring out of the open door.

Du Pré looked up at the Big Dipper. It was well past midnight.

There was nothing open in Cooper now but the saloon, nothing at all, and there really wasn't much open in Cooper past nine P.M.

So Nancy Wyman had taken Billie Pritchett someplace else. Maybe an early doctor's appointment in Billings.

The light went out and Du Pré watched the door slide to and the shadow of someone walking across the driveway. The door opened and closed on the truck, the engine ground a while and caught, and then the truck turned around and went down the ranch road toward the county road a half-mile or so away.

Du Pré rolled a smoke and lit it with the shepherd's lighter. He snuffed the glow in the rope by feel. He kept the cigarette in his cupped hand and his eyes closed.

When he had stubbed it out, he opened his eyes. Everything was as it had been. But whoever had been in the shed had left the light on. A glimmer showed under the door.

Du Pré went back into his trance and he stayed both awake and asleep until the light began to rise. Then he stood up and rubbed his legs for a time. He started back on the trail that went along the mountain.

It took him an hour and a half to get back to the cruiser. When he got close, he stopped and watched for a while before he came up to it. Nothing seemed to have changed.

Whatever was going on at the Pritchetts' could be right, or not.

I talk to Madelaine about it, Du Pré thought.

But if it is all right why am I here looking see my car has somebody in it, eh?

Nothing had moved. Du Pré went to the cruiser and got in. He started it and backed up to the main road and out on it and he went down toward the county road.

He drove to the bench road and along it to Benetsee's rutted driveway, and up that until he could lurch out of the ruts and park in the long yellow grass.

No one was there. The sweat lodge stood open and Du Pré looked at the ground as he walked around and there were no tracks but those of deer and coyotes. Lots of coyote tracks, but then the old man was brother to them.

Du Pré yawned. He was tired. He drove to Madelaine's and went in and showered and shaved and he got into the bed and went to sleep at once.

He woke when the door opened.

He swung his legs over the side of the bed and shook his head to clear it.

Madelaine appeared in the doorway.

"Ah," she said, "you are alone that is good. Big music star like you I think, I will find some groupie in bed with Du Pré."

"Yah," said Du Pré, "she jump out the window there, she is streaking through Toussaint but no one will notice."

"You been someplace," said Madelaine.

Du Pré yawned and nodded.

"I go and make coffee so I have Du Pré with his brain in his head to talk to," said Madelaine.

She went off. Du Pré pulled on his clothes and boots and he went to the kitchen and found her at the sink looking out into her backyard.

"Dry," she said.

Du Pré put his arms around her and she reached up and back to touch his cheek.

The water on the stove began to grumble just a little.

They stood like that until the water boiled and then they had coffee, in the cool kitchen. Outside it was hot and dry and mean.

"So this person you see," said Du Pré.

Madelaine nodded.

"Marsha," said Madelaine. "Pret' screwed-up kid, but she some few things. Say Beth and Willie are planning, run away, and they were afraid someone but Marsha don't know who. But Beth tell her she and Willie they are going to do something for somebody that is how they get the money to go with. But she don't know what. Marsha is not too smart and she was still pret' screwed up I talk to her, she has been in that place a month and she has trouble putting words on a string."

Du Pré nodded. He drank coffee.

"I go, the mountain back of Pritchett's place, watch, see Nancy Wyman push Billie, a wheelchair, to this van they go off I don't know where. Don't come back. But this truck come while they are gone, guy goes into the machine shed a while, goes away, I don't see who it is."

"Good," said Madelaine. "I go out there tomorrow maybe, see that Nancy."

"Don't look like there is no one else there," said Du Pré. "I don't see anyone move. But I am some up the mountain."

The wind began to pick up; leaves green but dry rattled in it.

"Damn," said Madelaine, "this is some weather, burn out the Wolfs maybe."

Du Pré nodded.

"I am here all my life it is never this bad," he said.

Madelaine went to the coffee and she poured some more and looked at Du Pré.

Du Pré shook his head.

"Maybe I go out there now," said Madelaine. "See that Nancy Wyman."

"Maybe they are not back," said Du Pré.

"OK," said Madelaine, "then we go, see Susan, I am still driving fast down the road."

"How is your car?" said Du Pré.

"Good," said Madelaine. "Let's go, the bar."

They walked so that Madelaine could stretch her legs.

There were a few people there, and Du Pré and Madelaine nodded and smiled and Susan came around the bar to hug her friend.

Du Pré had a ditch and Madelaine some pink fizzy wine.

"Some funny here," said Madelaine.

"Yah," said Du Pré.

"Everything it has burned or maybe it all will," said Madelaine, "there's a person setting fires to kill people, crazy person, who maybe lives here."

Du Pré nodded.

The door opened and the cop Vukovich came in. He took off his dark glasses and stood blinking for a while. He saw Du Pré and walked over.

"Hello, Madelaine," he said.

Madelaine nodded.

"You are back," said Du Pré.

Vukovich grinned.

"Can't stay away," he said.

"You know something," said Madelaine, looking at the cop.

"I do?" said Vukovich.

Madelaine nodded.

"Can't talk about it," she said.

Vukovich looked at Du Pré.

"Ongoing investigation," said Vukovich.

Madelaine looked at him.

She looked at Du Pré.

"I am gone a long time," she said.

Du Pré nodded.

"Finish your damn drink then," said Madelaine, "we got to go."

CHAPTER
30

Du Pré woke up and the light was rising. He could hear Madelaine in the kitchen, water running, then her moccasined feet on the floor.

He yawned and got up and went to the shower and then he dressed.

She was taking biscuits from the oven by the time he got to the kitchen. She put two of them halved on a plate and ladled rich sausage gravy over them. She put them in front of Du Pré.

"Ah," he said, and he ate.

"I am going, Cooper," said Madelaine, "need a few things the store and then I come back, maybe go out to Pritchetts'. What is for you this day?"

Du Pré shrugged.

He looked out at the light, bright now, filtered through the dust and smoke in the air. There were big fires raging all over the west and some of the burns were directly west. The sky would be white, not blue, and the light grew harsh and strained.

"The ironing," said Du Pré, "maybe I do that."

"Oh, poor Du Pré," said Madelaine, "poor fellow, he is not the big Du Pré today. He is feeling sorry, himself. You go find that Frazier and maybe that Vukovich drug cop."

Du Pré nodded.

"Lot of fires, Nancy Wyman's life," said Du Pré.

"Yah," said Madelaine.

"Damn Benetsee," said Du Pré.

"Him, gone," said Madelaine. "Him, Pelon, north."

"How you know that?" said Du Pré.

"Raven tell me," said Madelaine.

Du Pré nodded.

Madelaine went off to bathe and dress. Du Pré went outside and looked north toward the Wolf Mountains. They rose like shadows, behind the thick smoky dusty air.

Never see them like that. Never that pale, Du Pré thought, it is like they are ghosts there.

The door opened and Madelaine came out, her keys jingling in her hand.

"I be maybe till three, four," said Madelaine.

They kissed and she went off to her white Subaru. She backed it out and blew Du Pré a kiss as she drove away.

Du Pré cursed and went to his cruiser. He got his flask and had a snort and a smoke.

    . . . *feeling sorry for yourself Du Pré . . .*

Yes, me, I do, thought Du Pré, and there is something at Pritchetts' that stinks.

Me, I think I go back, the mountain.

Later. First maybe I see that Frazier, maybe Vukovich too.

Du Pré went into the house and put on his hat. He shut off the lights in the kitchen and went out to his cruiser and drove to the saloon.

Susan Klein was out in front, sweeping the board porch. She fished a beer bottle out from under one of the benches built into the wall and put it on the seat.

Du Pré grabbed it as he went in and he found a case of empties and dropped it in a hole.

Susan wasn't long in coming back. She took the big pushbroom to the mop closet, then came to her padded-backed stool behind the bar and made herself a tall clear soda and lime.

She sat, wearily.

"It is never hot in Montana at night, God damn it," she said.

Du Pré nodded.

It never had been, till now. Du Pré tried to remember another time when even the nights were hot. He couldn't.

Susan sighed. She got down off her stool. She reached across the bar and grinned at Du Pré. She grabbed his nose and she twisted pretty hard.

"There," she said, "it was all crooked."

Du Pré laughed.

"It is not that I am used to it," he said.

"Seen Benetsee?" said Susan.

Du Pré shook his head.

"Funny," she said, "Benny said he saw him late last night, walking by the road near his place."

Du Pré looked at her.

"That Frazier he is out back?" he said. Frazier had rented a room in one of the trailers behind the saloon.

Susan spread her hands.

Du Pré nodded and he went out the side door and around to the trailers. He went to the end room on the second one and rapped.

No answer.

He went to his cruiser and got in and roared off toward Benetsee's, driving faster than usual because he was angry.

This, one of his damn jokes I know, Du Pré thought.

He went up on the bench road and along it to the turnoff to

156

the old man's cabin. He bumped up the ruts and parked and got out and he walked to the door and banged on it.

No one home.

He went around back to the sweat lodge and it was as it had been.

He looked at the ground. Nothing.

He walked back to the cruiser, and near it he found a piece of blue plastic, just a fragment, small enough so he couldn't tell what it might have come from.

He walked back down the ruts.

He squinted.

There. A car or truck had driven up the track, and the driver had gone clear out away from the ruts at one point, risking tearing out the oil pan on one or another of the rocks that jutted up.

He went back to his cruiser and backed and went down the track very slowly. He could see the strange vehicle had gone to the right as it departed.

There were no tourists; the fires had driven them all away.

So who would come here looking for the old man?

Who Benny said he saw walking by the road.

But Benetsee was never seen like that.

And he did not walk on roads.

Not ever.

Du Pré pounded the steering wheel, angry. He finally wheeled and roared off west, toward the Pritchett place. He went up the same road he had gone on the night before last to the same side road and he went down it and parked in the same place.

He got out and changed back into the desert boots and he got the little backpack, adding clips for his nine-millimeter, already full of bullets. He took some jerky and fruit leather to have with the water. The sun was high and hot and the forest still and dry, crackling, ready to burn.

Du Pré trotted along the trail, down and around to the log over the cleft that still ran water: the little creek must have a source up so high it still held snowmelt. A few creeks did; the others had gone dry a couple of weeks ago.

The air was very still. The forest was so dry the needles of the firs and pines fell off if Du Pré brushed them.

It was hot. Du Pré slowed down. He was wearing a shirt with the sleeves cut off at the shoulder, and it kept him cool.

When he got to a good place he took out the binoculars and looked at the Pritchett place in the distance.

The van was there, and so was the old car.

Du Pré trotted along.

He got down to the vantage he had been at before, to the east of the house enough so he could see the two vehicles and the machine shed.

Locusts flew in the dusty light, but no birds called in the forest and even the squirrels, usually so quick to complain of intruders, were silent.

Du Pré picked up a handful of needles and crushed them in his hand. They crackled.

Jesus, it is dry.

I wait here for Madelaine I do not like this.

There is something there, ver' strange.

In that house.

The heat reached into the shade.

Du Pré took out his bottle of water and he drank some.

He rolled a smoke and carefully drew on it, his hand under it to catch any sparks.

The house stood silent.

Out across the plains to the south the haze had gathered so Du Pré could not see at all.

I wait here till Madelaine comes and is gone, then I go.

Then.

CHAPTER
31

The little white car came up the long road from the county gravel and Du Pré snapped awake.

Madelaine's Subaru.

She got close to the house and outbuildings and then Du Pré couldn't see her anymore. He looked at his watch.

Give her twenty minutes, then I go down.

But only fifteen passed, and then the little white car went back down the drive.

Du Pré sighed.

Have a nice-to-meet-you chat a glass of ice tea and then the old lady needs something so my Madelaine she gets up and she goes.

Madelaine's car turned left, headed for Toussaint.

I come here for nothing.

Du Pré stood up, rubbing his thigh muscles. Old injuries stitched and pulled and he counted his years and sighed.

Got, find me an apprentice like that Pelon, Du Pré thought, me I am old, like coal.

It was very hot and dry and breathless and Du Pré looked off to the west. The haze was thicker there.

Dry lightning coming.

Maybe the damn mountains burn all the way we don't got to worry anymore.

He began to walk slowly back toward the cruiser.

When he got to the place where he had stopped to look through the binoculars at the Pritchett spread each time on the way in, he took the Zeisses from their worn leather case and fastened them on the ranch and buildings.

He swung them south, and saw a roostertail of dust, a truck turning hard into the long drive.

Justin maybe. Old pickup.

The old truck came up the drive fast and it parked near the machine shed.

Justin got out.

Nancy, dressed now in denims and a straw hat, joined him.

Du Pré couldn't see her face, but he knew how she walked.

Justin and Nancy began to load things into the pickup.

Justin moved it away from the shed.

Du Pré kept the glasses on the open door of the machine shed.

The van pulled up.

The door in the side was away from Du Pré, but obviously they were loading the van, too.

Du Pré put away the binoculars and he began to trot back toward his vantage right above the ranch house and buildings.

When he got there he could see Justin and Nancy talking by the open shed door, standing inside just enough to miss the sun.

Du Pré ran down the hill and when he got to the house he crouched low and went under the windows to the west end of the house. He kept his head on the ground and, lying on his back, he very slowly pushed out far enough to see.

The machine shed was set so if they were still in it they could not see him.

Du Pré rolled and got to his feet and he ran toward a rusting hay baler that sat at the near end of the shed. When he got there he took out his nine-millimeter and put it in the clip holster and stuck it in the small of his back.

He waited.

He couldn't hear any voices, and then they were so close it was startling.

"Now," said Nancy, "it was supposed to be tonight, my lovely son, my darling, but now is when we have to do it. She knows. I know that bitch knows. I know she knows."

"We'll be *seen*," said Justin.

"Ah, but I have magic," said Nancy, "Now now now now now now . . ."

The last began as a trill and ended as a scream.

"All right, Mother," said Justin.

Nancy was humming, tunelessly.

She is some knotted up, Du Pré thought.

Nancy suddenly appeared, walking quickly toward the house.

Du Pré couldn't hear Justin, and then there was a *Damn* from inside the machine shed.

So what I do now?

Wait until they are gone find out what they are doing this machine shed here.

Nancy Wyman is nuts.

What they are doing they are doing now.

Du Pré heard the door begin to slide on its rollers.

He stood up and he stepped around the corner of the building. Justin was looking the other way.

Du Pré padded close.

"You," he said.

Justin jumped, turned, eyes huge.

Du Pré walked toward him.

"What is this?" he said.

"What are you doing here, Mr. Du Pré?" said Justin. "Jeez, you just fell outta the sky or somethin'."

"What is this?" said Du Pré. "Where is Billie Pritchett?"

"In the house," said Justin. "My mother went to get her. Take her for a ride, you know."

Du Pré looked at the kid, still white, shaking a little.

The front door of the house opened and Nancy Wyman pushed the wheelchair through it, drawing the door to with her hand. She looked over Billie, slumped and ancient in the hooded sweatshirt.

Nancy waved cheerily, and she expertly let the wheelchair down the ramp. She wheeled the old lady across the driveway toward the van.

The truck was clear across the way.

Du Pré smelled gasoline.

A tank up on a high frame stuck out on the other end of the machine shed.

Nancy Wyman trundled Billie Pritchett up to the van and she left her and she came on, a huge smile on her face. She was still in her denims. She was carrying something in her hand, it looked a little like a camera or a small radio or something.

"May I help you?" she said pleasantly.

"I am Gabriel Du Pré," said Du Pré, puzzled. "How is Billie?"

"Old," said Nancy, "very old. Would you like to say hello?"

Du Pré nodded.

They were about ten feet apart.

He walked toward her, and when he was close she lifted the thing in her hand and Du Pré's eyesight exploded, he reeled from a light so bright it froze him. He reached for his face and something hit him in the back of the head.

He fell to his hands and knees, blinded, and he was hit again and again.

When he woke he was in the back of the pickup truck, and it was bouncing over a dirt road.

Plastic jugs sat in the front of the bed, held by bungee cords.

The truck reeked of gasoline.

Du Pré couldn't see well, a bare blur.

He was well tied and lashed to one of the uprights in the rear posthole.

He tried to see more but his vision was clouded and grainy.

Then it faded again.

The truck slowed and turned.

Then it speeded up.

It hit a pothole and Du Pré flew against the bungee cords wrapped around his neck.

He couldn't move his hands or his feet.

They bounced on, slowed, stopped.

Doors slammed.

The tailgate went down.

"Mom!" said Justin. "There's his car! Over there!"

"God is very good to us," said Nancy, "very good very good."

They undid bungees, rolled Du Pré off the tailgate. He hit the ground hard.

A rope went around his bound feet and he could see Nancy and Justin straining on the ends, and they dragged him roughly down the side road toward the place he had parked his cruiser.

Part of his cheek scraped away on a rock.

"Get two of the flowers," said Nancy.

"In case one don't work?" said Justin.

"Get four," said Nancy. "We have to be very sure of this."

CHAPTER
32

Du Pré heard the van go. He still could hardly see and his eyes felt packed with sand. They were dry and the air stung them.

He was lying in a brush pile, one carefully gathered by Justin as Nancy danced and sang tunelessly, and when Justin was done Du Pré was trapped. He couldn't roll up and over the branches.

He strained and tried. His wrists and ankles were heavily wrapped with duct tape, his hands behind his back, and extra duct tape banded his thighs. He couldn't get enough purchase.

He strained and strained.

No use. All right then how I get this shit off me.

He heard a strange sound, slipping, wet, and then a roar. One of the gasoline bombs had gone off nearby.

He tried to roll again.

He felt with his hands for something sharp, but there was only brush.

He looked up at the sky, which shimmered white.

A faint smell of smoke came, and the sound of a fire rapidly growing and spreading.

The whole mountainside would be blazing in minutes.

Another wet hissing and explosion. And another.

Four of them, she had said.

The fourth is probably the one near me.

Du Pré strained again.

He heard something. A sound, behind the crackle and roar of the flames.

"Du Pré!" someone yelled.

The tape across his mouth was a little loose. Du Pré rubbed his face against a branch and it began to come off. Then it did, far enough for him to fill his lungs and yell.

"Here!" yelled Du Pré, his voice sounding feeble to him.

He tried to see around him and he couldn't.

"Here!" he yelled again.

A dog whined nearby, and then he heard someone running.

A knife slipped through the tape on his thighs and ankles and he rolled and his wrists came free.

"Up, come on," said Frazier, "we have to go now."

Du Pré couldn't see well at all. He tried to follow Frazier as fast as he could, but he kept stumbling.

Frazier finally swung Du Pré over his shoulder and began to plunge down the mountain.

Then he stopped.

"We're trapped," he said. "We'll have to go west."

"Is there a trail?" said Du Pré. "There is a creek over there, got this cut in the rock."

"Can you walk?" said Frazier. "Maybe if you grab the back of my shirt."

Du Pré wound his fingers in the loose cloth and Frazier set off.

When there was a log across the path Frazier would guide Du Pré over it.

The smoke was getting thicker and they were both coughing all the time.

Frazier picked up the pace and he pulled Du Pré along with him so fast that Du Pré would crash into him if he slowed or stopped.

They went on hacking and coughing while the fire boomed and banged around them.

Du Pré lost track of time.

There was just the running and stumbling and the smoke and the sounds of the fire eating the trees and duff.

Frazier began to go a little uphill.

They both gasped and puffed.

He began to go down a little.

Du Pré smelled something different.

Frazier stopped.

"This is it," he said. "I'll get in first, then you; I think it can hold us. If we can get enough air we might make it."

Du Pré sat down and waited until Frazier tapped his foot and then he inched forward and turned over to let himself down.

Frazier slipped and fell; Du Pré could hear him scrambling below, farther down in the rock cleft.

Du Pré waited. He was pressed between the rock walls, aware of the water rushing below, but he couldn't see well enough to move.

"Du Pré!" said Frazier, "move your right foot back about eighteen inches."

Du Pré did so, carefully balancing. He found a foothold and he put his weight on it. It was firm and pretty wide.

"Left about two feet," said Frazier.

Du Pré had to shift his weight and his hands felt very carefully for holds.

He moved and stopped.

"Down a foot on the left," said Frazier.

Du Pré felt with his foot.

He could see a little better, but not much.

Left.

Right.

Feel for handholds.

The fire roared and boomed closer.

Left.

Right.

Handholds.

"OK," said Frazier, coughing, "I'm going to grab your waist and swing you over and there's a place we can sit, sort of, here."

Frazier guided Du Pré's butt to a damp rock ledge, and he lifted first Du Pré's left foot and then the right and put them on another in front.

The water was gurgling and slowing a little, choked by ash.

The air was thinning and both Du Pré and Frazier were gasping. Du Pré turned toward him and leaned and he felt the rock on his cheek.

He felt something else.

A faint movement of air, sweet air, air without smoke in it.

"Here," said Du Pré. "Where my face is."

He could feel Frazier's breath on his face.

"My God," he said, "a miracle."

They breathed the breath of the mountain while the flames roared close and hovered over for a while, and then the flames were gone and the smoke thinned.

The fire rumbled away to the west and there was still a lot of noise as the knots in burning trunks popped.

"I'm going to go and see what's out there," said Frazier.

He moved off and was gone for several minutes.

Du Pré heard him come back, a few feet away.

"Du Pré," said Frazier, "if we can get you toward me six feet there's a place to get out of the cleft here. Damn water is gray grease."

Du Pré could hear it slopping over the stones.

Frazier guided him as he had before.

Then he grabbed Du Pré and pulled him up and Du Pré felt rock on either side of him and then nothing on his left, downhill.

"OK," said Frazier, "it's maybe a half-mile past us now, moving damn hard but not very fast. No big wind, thank God. But there will be one in a little while, forecasters said to forty-five miles an hour."

Du Pré's mouth was so dry his tongue stuck to his teeth.

"Grab my shirt again," said Frazier.

They moved on an angle downhill, since Du Pré still couldn't see.

The forest was hot, and when they passed a smoldering tree Du Pré could feel the heat radiating.

Du Pré fell and Frazier picked him up.

They went on.

Finally Du Pré felt the land flatten some.

"There's a fence up here," said Frazier. "The ranch burned but maybe I can find us some water."

He helped Du Pré through the fence.

They went on. Everything was still blurry to Du Pré, and he could make out only a vague shadow where Frazier was.

"Sit here," said Frazier.

Du Pré sat down.

The fire here smelled different from the fire in the forest.

He heard a helicopter *whock whock* overhead.

Frazier came back and sat by Du Pré.

"Here," he said. He gave Du Pré a big tin can.

Du Pré drank. It was wonderful.

He stopped.

"I hear a coyote just before you come," said Du Pré.

"Yes," said Frazier, "That was weird. Plain weird . . . I . . ."

"It is all right," said Du Pré. "I know."

CHAPTER
33

"Dumb shit," said Madelaine, "I am going, get Benny Klein to go on out there, see about Billie Pritchett, and you got to come, the big Du Pré, boom down the mountain, get the shit kicked out of you, and about burned up."

Du Pré nodded. His eyes were bandaged. He was sitting on a stool in the Toussaint Saloon with a ditch in his hand.

"Pret' dumb."

"You fuck up you do it good, Du Pré," said Madelaine, "Benetsee tell you leave this, Madelaine, you got to stick your big Métis nose in, can't be left out."

"Yah," said Du Pré.

"Benetsee save your sorry ass so many times," said Madelaine. "That Frazier he comes back early, thinks he'll just drive by Pritchetts', he knows about Nancy Wyman for sure now, he almost be there this coyote is in the road. Won't move. Frazier is pret' smart, so eventually the coyote, he goes up the road where Du Pré is."

"Yah," said Du Pré.

"Dumb shit," said Madelaine.

"Yah," said Du Pré.

"You get them, bandages off, I kick the shit out of you then," said Madelaine.

"Why you got to wait?" said Du Pré, "Won't be fair then either."

Men came in and went out, people from the fire crews, back to try to save the forest on the Wolf Mountains again.

"How you know I am coming there?" said Madelaine.

"You say so," said Du Pré.

"That is no excuse," said Madelaine.

"I am dumb-shit Du Pré," said Du Pré, "OK, and tomorrow I die. Maybe I have, me, another ditch."

Madelaine went off to get it.

She came back quickly.

Boot heels sounded on the old wooden floor.

"Du Pré," said Benny Klein. "You any better?"

"Yah," said Du Pré, "I am until tomorrow."

"So you want to tell me what happened?" said Benny.

Du Pré recounted the events at the Pritchett spread.

"That thing she used on ya is called a taser," said Benny. "I see 'em in cop-equipment catalogs. Supposed to quiet violent suspects right down."

"Yah," said Du Pré, "it would be good for that."

"They disappeared," said Benny. "No sign of either Nancy or Justin. We found the van she had, and the dummy in the wheelchair, just wood and rags. Billie Pritchett was buried behind the machine shed. Won't know for a while how long she's been dead."

"Truck?" said Du Pré.

"Found it, too," said Benny, "all burned up. Seems they went right around the Wolf Mountains. Setting fires. Maybe they had another car someplace. Hard to tell. The van and the truck was parked so they'd burn up when the fires began."

Du Pré nodded.

"Fire nuts," said Benny. "Sometimes they just run into the fires, I read."

Du Pré nodded.

"Crazy," said Benny. "You know Nancy Wyman lost her whole family in a fire. She was four, and her mother managed to throw her out of a window. It was winter and she landed in the snow, and watched her house burn down and heard her family screaming."

Du Pré nodded.

"Jesus," said Benny, "life can get hard."

Du Pré nodded.

"How the fires?" said Madelaine.

"We got three thousand men fightin' 'em again," said Benny. "After the winds last afternoon and night they was blowed up pretty good. Went to hell, it did. All the fighters can do is try and keep it away from ranch buildings. Lost a few summer cabins, over the other side. But it looks fair to burn out the Wolf Mountains. Frazier said that happened about three hundred years ago. I dunno how he can tell."

"You see him maybe say I like to talk to him," said Du Pré.

"Sure," said Benny, "He's around, I see him. Well, get well, I guess you can have them bandages off you tomorrow."

Du Pré nodded.

"Well," said Benny, "hope yer eyes is better soon. I got to be goin'. We barely saved the Lewis place and there's a couple others in a bad way."

Du Pré rolled himself a smoke and lit it and he passed it to Madelaine for her one drag.

In a while, Madelaine went and made cheeseburgers and fries for them both and they ate.

Du Pré was exhausted and so Madelaine took him home and put him to bed.

He dreamed.

Fires.

Billie Pritchett, tall and straight and whitehaired, walking her land or riding on her horse, Little John.

Sorrel with white socks.

Nancy Wyman's mad face floating in a pool of water, dissolving.

Justin Wyman, running away.

Du Pré slept fitfully.

He woke up and he touched the bandages on his eyes.

They were still there.

He sighed.

Goddamn things.

His eyes itched like hell. He stripped off the bandages. He kept his eyes shut and went to the bathroom and ran cold water and he bathed them. He opened them to slits.

He could see, faintly, the plug in the sink.

He shut the door and sat in the dark, looking at the light that came under the bottom panel.

Five minutes later he could see the bathroom pretty well, having very gradually opened his eyes. The bottom pane of the window was frosted and the top covered by a curtain. There was plenty of light, but it wasn't glaring.

His vision was still a little blurry, but not near as bad as it had been.

Du Pré went back to the bedroom and got dressed. He fished around in the drawer he kept his things in and found some dark glasses he wore only when the day was bright and snowy.

Madelaine was mixing batter in the kitchen, using an electric dingus.

She was a little time before seeing him.

"Ah," she said, "my Du Pré, he keeps the bandages on almost as long as the doctor says."

"My eyes they are pretty good," said Du Pré.

Madelaine nodded.

"The fires they are worse," she said, "but no wind is supposed to come now. So maybe they can do some little."

Du Pré nodded.

Madelaine pointed the spoon at him.

"You, are not going, help this time," she said.

Du Pré shook his head.

"Don't need that smoke, my eyes," said Du Pré.

"Where that Nancy, that Justin run to?" said Madelaine.

Du Pré sighed.

"Maybe they don't run," he said.

Madelaine looked at him.

"Maybe they are here. Some places in the Wolf Mountains they are safe. Up high, there is a lot of water, beaver, ponds, meadows, and the fire maybe don't reach up there. So they are up there and they wait a while."

Madelaine looked at him.

"What you know?" she said.

Du Pré shrugged.

"That Nancy, she is crazy," said Du Pré.

"Yah," said Madelaine.

"Justin is this kid, can't think for shit," said Du Pré.

"They find the van she is driving the truck," said Du Pré.

"Yah," said Madelaine.

"So they got another car maybe, I don't know," said Du Pré.

Madelaine nodded.

"My head aches," said Du Pré.

"Or there are three of them," said Madelaine.

"Yah," said Du Pré.

CHAPTER
34

Du Pré and Madelaine looked north to the Wolf Mountains, painted in fire.

Flames silhouetted peaks, red-orange curtains climbing in the black.

"That is it for them," said Madelaine.

"They die out, the grass comes back, the flowers, the trees," said Du Pré.

"Not while we are alive maybe," said Madelaine.

"People, they are alive only a little time," said Du Pré, "except for that Benetsee, who is five hundred years old."

"Him come back I wonder," said Madelaine, "his country it is burning he come back maybe."

Du Pré shrugged.

"Maybe," he said.

"Want to go look maybe?" said Madelaine.

"I get, come along," said Du Pré. "How nice, that, here I am just waiting, tomorrow, when you kill me."

Madelaine kissed him on the cheek.

"I let you live you behave some," she said.

Du Pré nodded.

"No more Du Pré bullshit," said Madelaine.

"Only kind that I got," said Du Pré.

They got up and went to Madelaine's little white Subaru and got in and Madelaine started the engine and she took off toward the bench road and Benetsee's.

The fires raged high on the mountains, but there wasn't any flame nearer than five miles, maybe more.

The cabin was dark and Madelaine pulled in to a patch of weeds and they got out and looked up at the mountain. A downdraft carried the stink of smoke to them.

"Old Man!" Madelaine yelled. "I am needing you here now! It is ver' dark and I cannot see!"

Silence. Then a great horned owl called, a soft hoot.

Something small scuttled through the dry grass.

They walked around the cabin and down the path to the sweat lodge. The door flap was up on top of the willow frame. Du Pré knelt and reached for the firepit.

"Cold," he said, "nothing here, long time."

"He is here," said Madelaine.

Du Pré sighed.

Benetsee, maybe he better be here. He knows what is good for him.

"Old Man!" yelled Madelaine. "God damn you, I am here, see you, you better come now. I got no time, this!"

The owl hooted.

Du Pré rolled a smoke. He sat on a stump and looked at the fires eating the mountain forest.

"Old shit," said Madelaine, "him, don't scare easy."

Du Pré snorted. He smoked.

A willow flute began to sound, liquid notes, so far off Du Pré couldn't tell if he was hearing it or imagining that he was hearing it.

The song ended.

The owl hooted.

Madelaine came and Du Pré moved over and she sat on the stump.

"He does this," she said, "gets people, do things, leaves, then they have to figure it out."

Du Pré laughed.

Benetsee, him do that, me, about four hundred times.

"But Du Pré, him always figure it out," said Madelaine.

Du Pré shook his head.

"Non," he said. "Me, I try, lots of times it is a disaster."

"This is true," said Madelaine, "but then you are just a man, not so smart as women."

I don't got nothing say, that one, Du Pré thought.

"Don't got nothing, say, eh?" said Madelaine.

"No," said Du Pré.

"It is here," said Madelaine, "not where we are maybe but it is all here, just can't see it."

Du Pré grunted.

"Just can't see it," said Madelaine, "like it is hard to see, the night."

"It is some dark," said Du Pré.

"Owl, him see good," said Madelaine.

"Got them good eyes, for the night," said Du Pré.

"For the dark," said Madelaine. "Night it is something else maybe."

Du Pré looked at her.

"Maybe everything but us see good, Du Pré. Maybe it is just not dark, maybe it is just us can't see," said Madelaine.

Du Pré looked at her.

"Sun, we see, we think we know," said Madelaine. "Night we don't see much, think we don't know."

Du Pré waited.

He thought he heard the flute sound again.

"Shit," said Madelaine, "old bastard, him be here maybe."

The owl was silent, and then there was a scream, a rabbit caught in talons.

Quiet.

The wind soughed.

Coyotes began to howl, songs Du Pré had never heard.

Fire songs maybe.

Coyotes, they watch the mountains burn many times.

"They have disappeared," said Madelaine.

Du Pré grunted.

"Nancy, Justin, they are gone," said Madelaine.

Du Pré looked at her.

"But maybe there is somebody else," said Madelaine.

Du Pré thought about the two bodies, the kids who were going to do something for somebody and then run away together.

McPhie.

The huge Highway Patrolman had said there had to be somebody else.

"In the night," said Madelaine.

"Meaning we cannot see them," said Du Pré.

"Because we are blind," said Madelaine.

"In the night," said Du Pré.

"So this person is here and doing this but we don't see them," said Madelaine.

Du Pré nodded. He had his flask in his pocket and he had a drink.

Madelaine shook her head.

"Old Man!" she yelled, "You better tell me, rest of the story!"

Du Pré laughed.

Madelaine got up and walked down to the creek. It ran clear and cold from a spring that burst up from the rock a mile or so away.

Madelaine walked along the path by the pool people plunged into after a sweat.

She stared down at the water.

"Du Pré come here," said Madelaine.

Du Pré got up and he went to her.

She pointed to the water.

There were faint reflections of the stars, and of Madelaine and Du Pré looking down, their shapes shimmering in the water's purl.

"There we are in the night," said Madelaine. "But there are stars."

Du Pré nodded.

The coyotes sang fire songs.

"Owl him in the night," said Madelaine. "Cree call them Hush Wings. You don't see owls much, the day, they live in the night."

"See them in the day there are birds after them," said Du Pré.

"They are there but they look like old bark, old branches, old stumps," said Madelaine.

Du Pré waited.

"This person, they do not look like what they are," said Madelaine.

Du Pré waited.

He nodded.

He thought he heard the willow flute again.

"Owl, him look like old bark, till it is night he can move, fly, hunt," said Madelaine.

Du Pré sighed.

"You hear that flute?" said Madelaine.

Du Pré listened, but again he couldn't tell whether the faint melody was in the air or in his brain.

"Son of a bitch," said Du Pré.

"Yeah, son of a bitch," said Madelaine. "Pretty good bark work, him."

The coyotes sang.

Madelaine looked at their reflections on the water.

"So it is that Frazier," said Madelaine.

"Yes," said Du Pré.

CHAPTER
35

Du Pré waited in the car while Madelaine went into the Toussaint Saloon.

She was back in a few seconds.

"Him not there, we check his room," she said. She got in and drove around to the trailers in back.

They got out and Madelaine went to the door of Frazier's room, and she used a key on her ring to open it.

They went in. Madelaine flicked on the light.

There were papers and clothes scattered on the floor.

Frazier had packed in a hurry and he was gone.

Madelaine looked at the stuff on top of the little desk.

She picked up a tape recorder. She turned it on. The tape whirred a while, there were sounds of people moving.

The bar.

Voices, laughter.

Du Pré looked at Madelaine.

"Son of a bitch!" he said. "Get them out of there, now—"

Madelaine shot through the door and she ran fast to the back door of the Toussaint Saloon. Du Pré came behind her, shining a flashlight on the cans and the shed-roofed entryway Madelaine had gone through.

The back door led to the big kitchen.

Du Pré looked around and then he went in, shining the light overhead, finding nothing in the open rafters.

He looked around the kitchen. People were moving out the front door.

"Out here Du Pré!" said Madelaine.

Du Pré came through the walkway and he looked at Madelaine who was behind the bar.

"Frazier, him leave this back here, ask Susan to watch it," said Madelaine.

An ordinary cardboard box, taped up.

"Get out," said Du Pré.

"Non," said Madelaine, "what we gonna do here?"

"Ask Susan, Frazier is carrying it how?" said Du Pré.

He knelt by the box.

He leaned over and looked all around it.

Plain cardboard.

Madelaine's running feet, she came to the bar and leaned over.

"Frazier say it is valuable crystal, him carry it like it is eggs."

"Valuable crystal," said Du Pré.

"So what we gonna do?" said Madelaine.

"I think," said Du Pré, "this maybe go off it is tipped any. Frazier think, well, sometime Susan wants to move it, pick it up, tip it, it goes off."

"OK," said Madelaine.

"So," said Du Pré, "I maybe pick it up, careful, walk it out across the street the empty lot."

"People out there," said Madelaine.

"OK," said Du Pré, "the back door then, but you got to tell me if there is anything, stumble over."

"Your big Métis feet," said Madelaine.

"I be a fucking ballet dancer," said Du Pré, "just this once."

He handed Madelaine the flashlight.

She came around the bar and she went down the short hall that led to the big kitchen.

"It blow up you run there is nothing you can do for me," said Du Pré.

"Ah," said Madelaine, "shut up."

Du Pré breathed deeply and he lifted the box very carefully and backed down the short hallway. When he got to the kitchen he turned around carefully so he could see where he was going.

"Nothing till there is this metal strip here the floor," said Madelaine.

Du Pré took seven careful steps.

Eight.

Nine.

"Six inches in front your right foot," said Madelaine. She was down the hall near the huge refrigerated locker. There was about six inches of clearance on each side.

Du Pré stepped over the strip. There was a doorway at the end of the linoleum that would be a tight squeeze.

"Walkway here it slopes," said Madelaine. "Then there is the outside door and the shed porch."

"OK," said Du Pré.

He walked on steadily and he put the box through the doorway, his sleeves touching the jambs. But he made it.

The floor was just plywood now, and it boomed a little when Du Pré's boot heels hit it.

Madelaine was outside now, and she held up her hand when Du Pré got near the threshhold and the single step.

"That thingus," said Madelaine, "the one step the ground."

Another tight doorway. Du Pré caught a cuff on the jamb. Madelaine reached in and freed it.

A step, another, and he was on the ground.

"Now it is clear, fifteen feet," said Madelaine. "Then there is this rut."

Du Pré stepped slowly ahead.

"Foot in front, your right foot," said Madelaine.

Du Pré stepped over the rut.

Madelaine kicked a beer bottle out of the way.

There was a grassy lot that was used as a place for people to park when the bar was very busy. There were three trucks there now. And then a barbed-wire fence.

"Me, I am not going, through the fence," said Du Pré.

"Rock there, go the right a little," said Madelaine.

Du Pré's arms ached. The box was not terribly heavy but the need to keep his arms in a single position was tough.

He got up to the fence and he set the cardboard box down. He heard the pickups start and move away.

Du Pré and Madelaine walked a hundred feet away.

The box sat on the ground, looking like an innocent cardboard box.

Du Pré saw Susan Klein.

"Don't let anyone go back in," he said. "This maybe is not the only one."

Susan nodded.

This Frazier is one sick bastard, Du Pré thought, but he is ver' smart.

A siren sounded and Du Pré turned.

The fire truck and the volunteers were coming down the street.

The truck pulled up in front of the saloon.

"What we got?" said a rancher, a helmet on his head, and cowboy from there down.

"Bomb maybe," said Du Pré, "I think this is one, maybe there is another."

"Sid!" said the rancher. "You take a look here."

The fire chief turned back to Du Pré.

"Sid was a SEAL," he said, "knows demolitions and booby traps."

Another man in cowboy boots and jeans and a helmet came walking up, easily, but covering the ground very fast.

"Anything else look out of place?" he said.

"I would know," said Madelaine, "Susan, too, maybe she take you in there."

The cowboy went off.

"OK," said Madelaine, "What about this thing?"

Du Pré shook his head.

"Blow the damn thing," said the fire chief. "Hell, shoot it."

Du Pré looked at Madelaine and he grinned.

She took out her funny nine-millimeter and she aimed.

Bang.

Nothing.

Bang.

Nothing.

"Shit," said Madelaine.

"Don't go near that," said Du Pré.

Somebody came up behind them, carrying a rifle with a telescopic sight.

Madelaine shot again.

Nothing.

Again.

The box turned into a flower of purple, red, and white.

There wasn't a huge explosion, just a vast bloom of flame.

It reached up and out and Du Pré and Madelaine stepped back.

The heat was intense for a moment and then it fell.

The cowboy who had been a SEAL went past Du Pré and Madelaine, carrying another box.

He set it down and he backed away.

The rancher with the rifle waited until the cowboy nodded.

Another bloom of flame.

"That one was set so a lot of people on the floor in front of the door there would set it off," said the cowboy.

"Jesus," said Du Pré.

"The bastard's good," said the cowboy.

"Oh, yes," said Du Pré.

CHAPTER
36

The Toussaint Saloon was full again. People had heard of the strange doings and they had come to see.

"Burn down my damn bar?" said one weathered man. " 'Bout frosts my cookies, that does."

The place had been searched thoroughly. The former SEAL had crawled around under the floor and gone through the attic and he had put a practiced eye to every place a bomb could be hidden.

"You sure?" said Du Pré to the man.

"I'm standing here having a stiff one," he said. "Don't think I'd do that I wasn't. I have seen people burned alive."

"Sorry," said Du Pré.

"Better to worry than not," said the man. "Now who the fuck is this prick Frazier?"

"Him a fire expert," said Madelaine.

"How nice," said the cowboy, "love and work, all together. Benny's after him?"

Du Pré nodded.

Benny and his deputies were looking round.

Madelaine jerked her head toward the door. Du Pré followed her outside.

"OK," she said, "where him go?"

Du Pré spread his hands.

"You go and dream," said Madelaine. "Come on I take you."

Du Pré shook his head.

"Maybe lots of places," he said. "But there is one maybe it makes sense he is at, maybe that Nancy and that Justin too."

Madelaine looked at him.

"Half Moon," said Du Pré.

"I hear of it never been there," said Madelaine.

The Half Moon mine was high in the Wolf Mountains. A little gold had come out of it, just enough to keep miners digging and hoping. But finally they ran out of hope and came down and the mine was still there, the bullwheels rusting on the ground, cables snaking all over, ore carts, red oxide boxes on tracks fallen away.

"Maybe there," said Du Pré. "There is a road, maybe not too good, comes up the north side of the Wolfs. Maybe there is a place to hide. Fires reach it, go in the mine, they pass pret' quick. There is water, it is hard to see from the air. Back in a blind canyon, steep, not much sun there."

"So," said Madelaine, "we go there maybe."

Du Pré looked at the fires raging on the mountain.

"You hunt mountain goats," said Du Pré, "Catfoot him tell me there is just this one good way hunt them."

"Ah, that Catfoot," said Madelaine, "he is one fine son of a bitch."

My papa. Yes, he is one fine son of a bitch.

"Mountain goat," said Du Pré, "him say goats are proud. They know that nothing climb higher than them."

Madelaine nodded.

"So you climb higher than them, come down from above they don't think anything is up there."

Madelaine nodded.

"So we take, helicopter up, have them drop us this side, walk over to the other," she said.

Du Pré nodded.

"The road, it is easy to watch," said Du Pré. "Winds up that last part, mountain across the canyon from the mine."

Madelaine nodded.

"So we get this helicopter fly us up there now," she said.

Du Pré shook his head.

"Them not flying much at night, tomorrow, early, they fly, noise seems like fighting fires maybe. But we got, walk up and over the top. Ver' rocky, still freeze up there every night. We got to go, maybe even we got the top wait until dark."

"OK," said Madelaine.

"Wait a long time," said Du Pré.

"Don't be givin' me bullshit," said Madelaine. "I wait as good as you, I wait good as anybody."

"OK," said Du Pré.

"Me, I don't go dream the damn deer. I got me Du Pré, go dream the deer shoot it," said Madelaine.

"OK," said Du Pré.

"Gut it all that crap," said Madelaine.

"You want to gut Frazier?" said Du Pré. "Fry him up maybe."

Madelaine ignored him.

"OK," she said, "so what we are going to need."

"This, painful for you," said Du Pré. "I make it easy as possible."

"Asshole," said Madelaine.

"OK," said Du Pré, "I shut up now."

"Yah," said Madelaine, "you just get the stuff together maybe I don't got to listen your bullshit, just go and get it ready I find us a helicopter."

"Bannerman," said Du Pré. Bannerman had a crop-dusting service, and two of his aircraft were helicopters.

"*Yes, Du Pré!*" said Madelaine.

Du Pré had another nice drink and then he left. He went to

his cruiser parked up by Madelaine's and he drove out to Bart's, where he had a room in the big house and a lot of gear in a tack shed near the barn.

He gathered backpacks and light sleeping bags and flashlights and a first-aid kit and odds and ends. He got some jerky and fruit leather from a sealed plastic box, slitting the tape and then taping the box shut again.

He drove back to Madelaine's.

She was in the kitchen, yawning. She had a cup of pale tea in front of her. Chamomile. Du Pré loved the faint sweet scent.

"Him, take us, ten," said Madelaine.

Du Pré nodded.

"You don't want, dawn, right?" she said.

Du Pré shook his head.

"Shit I am tired," said Madelaine.

"We get a good rest," said Du Pré. "Morning will be fine."

Madelaine nodded.

She went off to the shower and Du Pré made some tea for himself.

He sipped the scalding water, faintly flavored with chamomile.

Got a big horse pasture plant chamomile, fence it off, let it grow, want your horses, take down the gate, morning they will all be in there, very calm, them horses.

Du Pré was tired.

He thought of the bombs set at the bar.

If they had gone off Susan Klein and some other neighbors would be dead, burnt.

Like Lou Dykstra.

Someone banged hard on the door.

Du Pré cursed and he went to the front of the house. He opened the door.

The drug cop, Vukovich, was standing there.

"Where's fucking Frazier?" said Vukovich.

"I don't know," said Du Pré.

Vukovich looked at him a long time.

"OK," he said. "Thought you might."

Du Pré shook his head.

"Son of a bitch was under my fucking nose," said Vukovich, "and his name ain't Frazier. He's got a lot of names."

"He is crazy," said Du Pré.

"No shit," said Vukovich. "Crazy and a murderer."

The two men looked at each other a long time.

"I want him," said Vukovich.

Du Pré nodded.

"Bad," said Vukovich. "Lissen, you got not a hair's worth of authority. You fuck me up I'll bust you, bust you hard."

"Go get some sleep," said Du Pré. "Me, I do not like, threats."

"I fucking mean it," said Vukovich.

"Me, I do too," said Du Pré.

Vukovich's eyes were red and he rubbed them.

"Remember," said the drug cop.

Du Pré shut the door.

Madelaine was standing behind him.

"Him, pissed off," she said.

Du Pré nodded.

"Frazier is not Frazier he says," said Du Pré.

Madelaine looked at him.

"Him all the Frazier I need," she said.

CHAPTER
37

The helicopter jumped up as a thermal from the fires below caught the rotors.

Bannerman looked over and grinned.

"Whoop de dooooooo!" he yelled.

"Fuck," said Madelaine, strapped in the seat beside the pilot.

Du Pré was scrunched up behind them. It was a small helicopter, and usually carried just Bannerman and his insecticides.

There was a faint odor of petroleum distillates in the cockpit.

"Where ya want exactly?" yelled Bannerman.

Du Pré pointed to a triangular peak slightly to the left.

"Either side there," he said, as loud as he could.

Bannerman corrected the course.

In three minutes they were getting close.

Bannerman looked down, searching for a place he could land safely.

He hovered and then went west and dropped down to a flat

ridge that stuck out from the peak. There was a place on it, covered in alpine flowers and tiny willows, that had fewer rocks than most.

Bannerman set the helicopter down and he switched the engine off and they waited while the rotors wound down.

Then they all got out. Du Pré hauled out the backpacks, each with a sleeping bag hung from the bottom.

Bannerman looked at the fires raging below.

"You sure you wanna do this?" he said.

Du Pré nodded.

"Want me to come and check on you?" Bannerman said.

"Tomorrow," said Du Pré. "You know where Half Moon is? You see a lot of white smoke you set down, you get Benny to get people up there right away."

Bannerman nodded.

"I am not sure there is anyone there," said Du Pré.

"Well," said Bannerman, "I'll check for white smoke and do like you said."

He would, too. He had a word.

Du Pré and Madelaine moved away from the little helicopter, and Bannerman started the engine and in a moment he lifted up and was gone, fluttering down the mountainside.

Madelaine watched him go.

She looked at the peak above them. It had steep slopes and very sharp ridges running east and west.

Broken scree lay in huge fields.

"Fuck me runnin'," said Madelaine. "We, walk up over that."

"Yah," said Du Pré.

"Shit," said Madelaine, "why I do this to myself."

"You are tough Métis lady," said Du Pré.

"Maybe they are not there," said Madelaine.

"Maybe not," said Du Pré.

"You dream them?" said Madelaine.

"*Non,*" said Du Pré.

"Just a maybe good idea?" said Madelaine.

"Yah," said Du Pré.

"When me, I see that Benetsee," said Madelaine, "I am going to kill him. I use a shovel. I want to hear it go bang bang on his mean old head."

"Yah," said Du Pré.

"Old son-of-a-bitch bastard," said Madelaine.

"You are getting to know, Benetsee," said Du Pré.

"OK," said Madelaine, "I got him to kill, me, I can live through this."

She lifted up the packs.

She swung the heavy one onto her shoulders.

"Non," said Du Pré, "me, I take that."

Madelaine shook her head.

"I take the light pack you make for me I don't hurt so much I maybe don't really want to kill Benetsee, this way, him dead."

"OK," said Du Pré.

"We go now?" said Madelaine.

Du Pré nodded.

He looked at the routes up and around the peak.

"We camp tonight up there," he said.

"OK," said Madelaine.

"Go over couple hours before dawn find cover, wait," said Du Pré.

"Why we don't go over right after dark, find cover, wait down lower," said Madelaine.

"OK," said Du Pré.

"So," said Madelaine.

Du Pré led the way along the ridge to the flank of the mountain, and he found a goat trail that went to the east. He went along it. It was a good trail and it led them through the scree field to another ridge, one that ended almost at the saddle between the high peak and the next one to the east.

They walked, steadily, for an hour, and made good time.

Du Pré stopped and they sat and rested. They were both breathing hard. The air was thinner up here.

"Not too bad," said Madelaine.

In a few moments they went on. The trail got steeper and soon they were walking up a hundred feet and stopping for five minutes.

The saddle didn't seem to be that much closer.

"Long damn way," said Madelaine.

A sudden gust of air came roaring down from the peak. It was so hash that Du Pré and Madelaine huddled in the lee of a slab of rock until it fell away.

"So he could not drop us no higher," said Madelaine, "we are all a greasy spot on this rock."

They went on.

A hundred or a hundred and fifty feet, and then a rest.

The trail was zig-zagging now, as it wound up to the crest of the ridge.

Du Pré offered to take the heavier pack but Madelaine would not give it up.

They stopped and had some fruit leather and water.

Madelaine ate four big pieces.

"Good stuff," she said. "I make this for you yes?"

Du Pré nodded.

The sugar gave them strength and they went on.

It took the rest of the afternoon to get to the saddle. Du Pré found a flat place where they could sit with some comfort. The rocks were cold.

"Gets damn cold up here, yes?" said Madelaine.

"Yah," said Du Pré.

"He maybe don't see us in twilight anyway," said Madelaine.

"No," said Du Pré, "we just got to be careful. Can't use the lights much, have to make sure the beam is not toward the mine."

"Let's go, the top, go over soon as we can," said Madelaine.

They put on the packs, Du Pré taking the heavy one this time. Madelaine said nothing.

In an hour they were at the top of the saddle, looking down a scree slope that stretched hundreds of yards down the mountain.

"That is a trail," said Madelaine. She pointed to the faint track in the broken rock. The trail went swiftly down. The slope wasn't as steep on the north side of the mountain.

There were some stunted trees perhaps two miles away. And below them, thicker stands.

Du Pré took out his binoculars and he trained them on the narrow canyon that the Half Moon mine was in.

He looked for a long time.

"You see anything?" said Madelaine.

Du Pré nodded.

"Point these there," he said.

Madelaine stared through the binoculars.

"Ah," she said, "that is a fire."

"Yes," said Du Pré.

"Long way from the forest fires."

"Yes," said Du Pré.

"I just see the light dancing," said Madelaine.

Du Pré handed her the case and she put the binoculars in it and put them in her pack.

They waited until the light failed and then they went over and down the trail they had seen earlier.

It was tough going.

"It is harder going down than going up," said Madelaine.

"Yah," said Du Pré, "it is, that."

"How come you don't tell me?" said Madelaine.

"I am keeping my mouth shut," said Du Pré.

"You, Benetsee, both die," said Madelaine.

CHAPTER
38

Madelaine brushed a sweaty lock of hair from her forehead. She took the binoculars from Du Pré and she trained them on the narrow canyon a couple of miles away.

They had walked through the cold night, Du Pré leading the way, shining a shrouded flashlight behind him to help her see the rocks.

The moon had come up late and it gave a pale light. The dancing fire at the old mine had died down.

"So what we do now?" said Madelaine.

"Go on in maybe you can walk more," said Du Pré. "When we get to the canyon, me, I go ahead maybe sixty, eighty yards. Frazier he maybe expect me. He don't maybe expect anyone coming a little behind."

Madelaine nodded.

"OK," she said, "he is going to shoot you maybe?"

Du Pré shook his head.

"Him crazy," he said. "I think he want, talk at me."

Madelaine nodded.

"OK," said Madelaine, "but I got to think, sometime here."

She shut her eyes and she began to move her lips.

Praying.

Du Pré kept his eyes on the cleft in the mountain.

Nothing moved, nothing changed.

Madelaine stayed silent for fifteen minutes, and then her eyes opened.

"Non," she said softly.

Du Pré looked at her.

"I go in first, me, you come behind," she said.

"Non," said Du Pré.

They locked eyes.

"Old people tell me something I do not understand," said Madelaine, "but me, I know it now. You got to trust me, Du Pré."

Du Pré clenched his jaw.

He hit his thigh with his fist.

"It is dangerous," he said.

"Yah," said Madelaine. "So?"

"You got to let me," said Du Pré.

Madelaine reached out and she touched Du Pré's cheek.

"No, Du Pré," she said. "You got to *let* me."

Du Pré looked at the cold pale moon far away.

He shut his eyes.

He nodded.

"OK," she said, "we go now. You stay back, we go slow, it is a couple hours to the light now."

She stood up and put the backpack on. Her breath plumed in the cold air. The sky behind the mountains to the south flared red and mean.

Du Pré stood up and they went on, and there was enough light now so that he didn't use the flashlight.

The trail wound back and forth down the mountain. It was

steep and slow going, for they had to walk many yards to make one yard downhill.

There was a dry watercourse at the bottom, which would run high with snowmelt in the spring. Now there wasn't even a scent of water.

They started up toward the cleft in the mountain, and soon came to the road, cut and furrowed by the years of runoff. Du Pré flicked on the light. There were tire tracks, from motorcycles.

"Dirt bikes," he said. "Them, they can make it up here. Against the law, maybe they get a ticket."

He was whispering, his lips close to Madelaine's face.

Keep the sounds low when you hunt.

Whispers.

Night.

Du Pré went on up the road, keeping his eyes on the shadows black in the narrow canyon.

There was nothing.

In half an hour they had come to the place where the road went into the dark. There was no flickering ahead, nothing at all. They went into shadows and sat, listening.

Du Pré heard something. It was faint, so faint he couldn't tell what it was, only that it was there.

"I hear it," whispered Madelaine, "almost and then not."

"OK," said Du Pré, "you still want to do this?"

"Got to," said Madelaine. "Now I am seeing, maybe what it was they said, the sweat lodge."

Du Pré didn't say anything. He looked up at the moon and nodded. He took his nine-millimeter out of the pack and checked it and racked a shell into the chamber. He put the hammer down. It was a combat pistol and had no safety.

Madelaine didn't get her gun out.

She leaned over and kissed Du Pré and she walked up the road. The moonlight glinted on her hair.

Du Pré followed, darting from deepest shadow to shadow. There was just a little light in the canyon.

Madelaine walked up the center of the road, her hands in her jacket pockets.

Du Pré cursed. She wasn't using what cover there was.

But there was nothing he could do.

The road rose quickly. There were rusted rails on a narrow bed cut into the mountain. Once there had been a short rail here, a donkey engine above pulling little cars up with a cable, sending down high-grade ore to wagons, or to the underpowered trucks of the 1920s.

Du Pré hadn't been to the Half Moon for forty years, not since Catfoot had brought him.

Madelaine stopped for a moment.

Du Pré did, too.

He could hear it now.

Singing.

A person singing, a lilting melody.

"La lalala lala la lalalala . . ."

It was no song that Du Pré knew at all. He had to force himself to stay back.

Madelaine walked on, steadily, her head down a little, her stride even.

Du Pré kept dashing from cover to cover. He wished he had cork for his face.

Madelaine went around a spur of rock.

Du Pré ran hard to get there. He stopped, breathing hard.

The song went on.

"La lalala lala lalalala . . ."

Du Pré got down on the ground and looked carefully around the spur.

Madelaine was more than a hundred yards ahead now.

The canyon had opened up.

There was a flat place, and the crumpled mine works.

A person, naked, was dancing loosely, swooping around in a circle.

Singing, singing.

Du Pré stood and he trotted on.

Madelaine kept walking at the same pace.

Du Pré caught up to her.

They stopped and looked at Nancy Wyman, dancing and singing in the moonlight.

Someone sat on an old ore cart, head in hands.

A body lay on the ground, facedown.

Madelaine and Du Pré walked on.

"La lala lalalalala," sang Nancy Wyman.

They came to the body.

Frazier. He was dead and had been for a while.

Justin sat on the ore cart with his head in his hands. A little pistol lay on the ground near his feet.

Madelaine went to him and she put a hand on his shoulder.

He didn't look up.

"I didn't know what to do," he said.

His mother sang.

Madelaine picked up the pistol.

"I killed him," said Justin. "All this started because of him."

"Non," said Madelaine, "it started longtime gone."

Justin began to sob.

Nancy danced in the cold moonlight, naked.

"La lala lalalala lala . . ."

Du Pré rolled a smoke and lit it.

The five people were still in the moonlight.

Du Pré's glowing coal moved, and so did Nancy, again.

"La lala lalalala lalala . . ."

CHAPTER
39

Du Pré pulled the spruce branches out of the pool of water that stood in a pit near the mine mouth. He dragged them to the fire ring, coals held by stones. He put them on top of the red glow and the water hissed and white steam and smoke rose in a whorl.

He looked at the sky. No sign of Bannerman. But he would be along.

Du Pré was wreathed in choking fog, and he coughed and backed away.

He rolled a smoke and lit it and he sighed. He was bone tired. No sleep and lots of walking.

Madelaine and Justin and Nancy Wyman were all sitting in the shade of a collapsing building, perhaps the old livery stable. Madelaine had soothed Nancy enough so she was able to dress her, and the madwoman sat quietly, staring off to a third world of the mind, the place she lived in now.

Justin was slumped, asleep, his head held up by silver boards.

Du Pré watched the smoke column. It would keep on for perhaps fifteen minutes. Then he would have to pile on more boards and thin tree limbs, to get a quick burn for the head. There were still a dozen boughs soaking in the pool.

Madelaine went to a spring trickling from a rock face and she filled a plastic bottle with water. The top had been cut away and it was like a big glass.

She carried it over to Nancy and put it to the woman's lips and tilted the bottle gently. Some slopped on the front of Nancy's shirt, but Du Pré saw her throat moving, too.

Frazier's body lay where he had fallen. Du Pré had thought of covering him over, but the police would have to look at Frazier and the earth around him carefully.

Frazier was swelling in the rising heat.

Hope we get a ride before he pops like a balloon, Du Pré thought.

He looked up again and saw the little helicopter coming over the mountains. Bannerman flew straight down to the mine, dodging through the narrow canyon. He hovered overhead for a moment and then he rose and went back over.

Du Pré pulled the branches off the fire and let them burn out on the rocky ground. The heat shimmered above the coals but they would not last much longer. It was a good fifty yards to the nearest tree, and there was no wind.

Du Pré didn't bother carrying water to the dying fire.

Madelaine had quit trying to feed water to Nancy. She looked at Du Pré and shook her head.

Justin was snoring.

Madelaine got up and walked over to Du Pré. She dumped the water from the bottle.

"So," she said, "him see you?"

Du Pré nodded.

"How long till they come I do not know," he said.

There were fires down below, and airplanes and helicopters fighting them.

Maybe they could walk down, maybe not, but Nancy was in no shape to do it.

"Some big mess eh?" she said.

Du Pré nodded.

"Frazier save your life once, he liked you," said Madelaine.

Du Pré nodded.

"Don't know why he liked me," he said. "He is a man didn't like anyone he could not use I think."

"Had to be him all along," said Madelaine. "Pret' smart that."

Du Pré nodded.

"You are likable fellow," said Madelaine. "Good thing."

"That Justin he say anything to you?" said Du Pré.

"Just that he shoot Frazier one time the back of the head. But he don't say why. I don't know how long this went on."

Du Pré shook his head.

"Nancy she kill Maddy Collins," said Du Pré. "Maddy, she is calling for Billie Pritchett, won't take no more excuses Billie she can't come, the phone."

"Or Frazier," said Madelaine.

"*Non,*" said Du Pré, "Frazier he get people do things. Him stay in the shadows."

"Night," said Madelaine.

"You didn't have, shoot anybody," said Du Pré.

"You, Benetsee, soon as it is time," said Madelaine.

Du Pré sighed.

"It is not fair," he said. "If me, I get to shoot Benetsee and then you shoot me it is fair."

Madelaine grinned at him.

"Life is not fair," she said.

Du Pré nodded.

Nancy was singing again.

"Lala la lalalalala lala . . ."

Justin woke, squinted, and looked around as though he did not know where he was. He stood up.

He walked to the spring and he drank and put water on his head.

His shirt was dark with sweat.

"What they do to him?" said Madelaine, "Put him that Deer Lodge?"

Du Pré shrugged.

"Don't know how many people he kill," said Du Pré. "They count them up then they maybe know what to do."

"Jesus, what a mess this is," said Madelaine.

Du Pré nodded.

"Funny story yes," he said. "Don't know we know it though."

Madelaine looked at him.

"Someday maybe," said Du Pré.

There was the sound of rotors and a huge olive-drab military helicopter lumbered slowly over the saddle that Du Pré and Madelaine had walked over. The helicopter halted in the air and then moved ponderously toward the narrow canyon.

The engines and rotors were very loud. It was a huge machine.

Du Pré looked around the flat place near the mine mouth.

Maybe big enough, maybe not.

The machine appeared overhead and hovered and a cable came out of the side door and a man in uniform threw out a basket stretcher.

The cable lengthened and the stretcher touched the ground with one end and then it lay flat. A man dropped out of the helicopter door and slid rapidly down the cable and another man came right after him.

The first soldier unclipped his safety line and dashed over to Du Pré and Madelaine.

"What we got here?" he said.

"One dead, one crazy, one maybe crazy," said Madelaine. She pointed at Justin and Nancy. "You want me, go in the helicopter, knock them both out and tie them up good."

The soldier nodded.

He took a small phone from a pocket on his thigh and spoke a few words as he walked toward Nancy and Justin Wyman.

The second man had come down and he walked toward them, too.

They both glanced at Frazier but they didn't slow down.

Justin was sitting again, his head in his hands.

One of the soldiers knelt by Nancy. He took a syringe out of a kit and he broke open a sterile swab. He gave her a shot.

The other man was talking to Justin, who stood up and turned around. The soldier handcuffed him.

He left Justin then and he went to his partner and Nancy, who was sagging, and together they carried her to the stretcher and put her in and signaled and the cable tightened and the stretcher went on up to the helicopter and was pulled in.

In a few moments the stretcher was lowered again, and the soldiers led Justin to it and strapped him in, adding a strap around his ankles when he lay flat. One bent to ask him something but Du Pré and Madelaine couldn't hear what.

The basket was lifted.

"You're next," said one of the soldiers.

Madelaine went up. Then Du Pré. The soldiers came up together.

Frazier still lay on the ground.

The huge helicopter lifted and then went down the slope of the mountain. They crossed forests of ashes, and then they were out over the plains. The fires were now east and west, hot and moving.

It was too noisy in the helicopter to talk.

Justin started to buck, and one of the medics sat on him.

Madelaine put her head on Du Pré's shoulder.

He touched her cheek with his hand.

CHAPTER
40

"Vukovich," said Madelaine, "I am going to make you sorry you ever draw breath. You are a stupid prick. You got crab lice for brains. I am, me, going to rip your fucking head off, shit down your windpipe."

The tan government sedan shot along the highway. Vukovich and another agent, who was driving, stared straight ahead.

"Asshole," said Madelaine. She squirmed, trying to find comfort in the backseat, with her hands cuffed behind her.

"Ya interfered," said Vukovich. "Ya knew stuff and ya din't tell me. Knowledge of felonies, knowledge a the whereabouts of Frazier and the Wymans. I tol' ya not to fuck with me. Ya fucked with me."

"Bullshit," said Madelaine. "Me, Du Pré, we don't *know* nothing."

"Oh, ya," said Vukovich, "it's why you just get a lift, toppa the fucking mountain, so you can sneak up on Frazier, who is dead thanks to you, and the Wymans. Ya knew they was there an' I tol' you not to interfere."

"We did not know they were there," said Madelaine, "it was all a big maybe."

"Tell it to the goddamn judge," said Vukovich.

"Yah I will," said Madelaine.

"Give ya a hint. Watcher mouth. Ya talk to him like ya do to me ya'll be inna can for contempt about forty years," said Vukovich.

"There is that Pompey's Pillar," said Du Pré, looking off to the right. The odd sandstone formation sat down near the Yellowstone River, behind a fence. It had a lot of graffiti on it.

They drove on into Billings and to the federal building. The driver stopped at a side entrance.

A man in his sixties, with an expensive suit and a brush cut, came out of the door.

Vukovich looked at him as he got out.

"Gotta coupla prisoners stick inna cell," he said. "Where is the cell this place."

The gray-haired man cleared his throat.

"Um," he said, "you and I need to talk." He nodded at the parking lot, and Vukovich's face turned deep red.

"Go on," said the gray-haired man, "I'll catch up to you."

Vukovich walked slowly away, bouncing on his toes with each step.

"Breeden," said the gray-haired man, "get the goddamn cuffs off these people. Mr. Du Pré and Ms. Placquemines, my apologies. Vook is a fine agent with a short temper."

"He is a fucking asshole," said Madelaine.

But the gray-haired man was walking swiftly after Vukovich.

Breeden opened the door on Madelaine's side and he unlocked her cuffs. She rubbed her wrists and she got out. Du Pré waited until Breeden opened the door and freed him, and he got out, too, rubbing his wrists.

"Look," said Breeden in a low voice, "for what it's worth, I thought he was wrong. But I am only a humble spear-carrier."

Du Pré looked across the parking lot.

Bart was standing next to a huge SUV. There were two young men in steel-framed spectacles and elegant suits standing with him. The briefcases were soft leather, the expressions those of bored, well-bred cobras.

Bart was wearing rusty-colored overalls and a feed-store hat.

"Come on," said Madelaine, "my wrists get better I kill and scalp that goddam Vukorich."

"Yah," said Du Pré, looking off toward Vook and the gray-haired man, "I think it is happening now, you don't got to do nothing."

"Wanna ride home?" said Bart. "All modern conveniences."

"Got a machete?" said Madelaine.

"Not for you I don't," said Bart. "Bill, Dave, thank you much."

The two lawyers nodded and they strode away.

"Thanks," said Du Pré.

"Least I could do," said Bart. "Can't have my friends caught in the toils of federal justice."

"I want that Vook's nuts," said Madelaine.

"Nah," said Bart. "Fuggedaboudit."

"What?" said Madelaine.

"God, fuggedaboudit," said Bart. "Leave it, fer Chrissakes."

Madelaine smiled at him.

"No," she said.

"Madelaine," said Bart, "castrating, killing, and scalping a federal agent—well, it upsets them. They get mad. There's no end of trouble. So if you won't forget about it *shut the fuck up about it*! I went to a lot of trouble to make this go away."

Madelaine smiled sweetly at him. She kissed his cheek.

"Pink wine you maybe got?" she said.

"Sure do," said Bart, "whiskey for Du Pré, good salami and cheese and fruit and stuff. We could leave right now. I got a foundation hole to dig yet today. Gordon's supposed to set forms in the morning."

Du Pré laughed. My rich friend who digs holes.

Madelaine opened the back door of the SUV and she looked in.

"Ah," she said. "There." She stepped up and sat on the plush seat and she lifted up the cooler lid.

She pulled out a jug of pink fizzy wine and found a paper cup and had some.

"OK," she said, "I let him live."

Du Pré and Bart got in the front seats.

Bart started the engine. It made no noise at all. He drove to a ramp and they were passing Pompey's Pillar soon enough. The turn north wasn't all that far, a hundred miles or so.

Bart put on a tape of Celtic fiddling. Du Pré sipped whiskey and he nodded in time to the music.

"Sorry it took so long," said Bart over his shoulder. "I had to fly down here, and the lawyers had to come up from Denver."

"It is all right," said Madelaine. "It is over now isn't it?"

"You still got to kill me, Benetsee," said Du Pré.

"I am too tired," said Madelaine, yawning. "I would miss you two bastards I killed you. No one to talk to." She yawned again. She fished a pillow out from behind the seat and settled herself and she soon was snoring a little.

"Some people can get damn lost," said Bart.

Du Pré nodded.

Nancy was lost, and Justin had gotten lost with her.

Seventeen-year-old kid, maybe eighteen; now he would do hard time.

"How the hell did this all start?" said Bart.

"Longtime gone," said Du Pré. "Fires then fires now."

Bart nodded.

Du Pré began to whistle a strange melody. It rose and looped and fell and rose.

He tapped his fingers on the dash for time.

"What was that?" said Bart, when Du Pré had stopped.

"Fire song," said Du Pré, "coyotes sing it. I never heard it until these fires, so it is their fire song."

"It's eerie and sad," said Bart.

Du Pré nodded.

The Great Plains rolled away to the east, the horizon purple in the sun.

"I think I know how whoever the guy was called himself Frazier got to Nancy. Computer. She was taking care of Billie Pritchett, bored out of her skull. I heard agents were hauling stuff out of Pritchett's place. I bet the whole story is on it."

Du Pré shook his head.

"Not this time," he said, "there is too much. There is the fires, who is setting them. There is that Frazier, whoever he is. There is the drugs."

Bart nodded.

"Burning up the country here," he said, "methamphetamine."

"Yah," said Du Pré, "it is hard stuff that."

"Billings is about eaten alive, I guess," said Bart.

Du Pré rolled a smoke and lit it and crouched close to the little slit in the window, so the smoke drew out.

"I don't mind it," said Bart.

"So," said Du Pré, "crazy people, crazy woman, but it would not have been so bad, that damn computer like you say."

Bart laughed.

"Yah yah yah," he said, "I know you hate the things."

Du Pré nodded.

"So," said Bart, "the Wolf Mountains will be about burnt out."

"They come back," said Du Pré.

"Take some time," said Bart.

Du Pré looked at the vast and spare land.

"It got plenty of time," said Du Pré.

He started to whistle the coyote's fire song again.

CHAPTER
41

Du Pré and Bassman and Talley finished "Coyote Fire Song." The huge crowd in the field across from the Toussaint Saloon was utterly silent. Most of the audience were firefighters, young and tough, who'd spent weeks on the fireline without a break.

Then they began to clap and whoop and roar.

Du Pré and Talley and Bassman bowed, and they set their instruments down and left the stage, a boxy thing cobbled together from old plywood and framing lumber. The sound system was gigantic, and had been rented from a firm in Minnesota.

Susan Klein had bought a thousand T-shirts with "1st Ashstock Festival" lettered on the front, and a weary firefighter holding a Pulaski on the back.

A rock band from Missoula played next.

There was still forest on the Wolf Mountains, but much of the timber had burned. There had been a couple of rains, and fireweed glowed on the flanks of the mountains, brilliant pink in the ashes.

"Damn that is one fine song there," said Bassman, "them coyote they sing pret' good."

Du Pré nodded. He put his arm around Madelaine, who was lovely in her silks and silver and turquoise.

A long rank of trestle tables off to one side held vast pots and containers of beans and salads, and two of them had ranchers slicing barbecued beef and lading plates. It was all free for the firefighters. They would leave in the morning, in the trucks and buses painted with their names.

Hot Shot teams from reservations, from southern states, from all over the country. There were even some Australians. It had been a hell of a season, a fire war.

Du Pré had a long pull on a big ditch highball. The whiskey and ice and water tasted fine. He rolled a smoke and let Madelaine have her first long drag. She never took any more.

"So it is pret' good after all," said Madelaine.

Du Pré looked up at the Wolf Mountains, ash and blue, snow on the peaks. Late August and winter had come up there, and this morning the northwest wind had smelled of fall.

"Yah," he said, "fireweed, pret' stuff that."

Up from the ashes.

Du Pré looked round, over at the buses and trucks parked in long ranks in the pasture that also was the airfield. The windsock hung limp, but in an hour or so a little wind would come down from the Wolf Mountains and then it would dance.

Du Pré saw two people standing in the shadow of the shed that covered the side door of the Toussaint Saloon.

Benetsee and Pelon.

"Ah," said Du Pré, nodding toward them, "there is that old son of a bitch you need to kill, him."

Madelaine looked.

She grinned evilly.

211

"We go, talk to them," she said. "Me, I leave my gun at home. I think maybe there is a shovel there, side door. Snow shovel. It will take a long time kill him with that."

They walked across the road.

Benetsee and Pelon smiled at Madelaine and Du Pré.

"Old Man," said Madelaine, "I am some mad, you. You tell me, do this, you don't tell me how."

Benetsee laughed, an ancient cackle.

"I, me, cannot do ever'thing for you. You plenty smart woman, you listen, the old ones, it will be all right," he said.

Madelaine stopped in front of him.

She bent over and kissed him on the cheek.

"Phew," she said, "old son of a bitch you need a bath pret' bad."

"Du Pré," said Benetsee, "your woman here needs, shut up."

Du Pré ignored him.

"Come on, damn it," said Pelon, "I need one, too."

"Clean clothes, the plastic trunk hall closet," said Madelaine. "Pelon, maybe you just boil this old bastard."

"Shit," said Benetsee. But he trudged off toward Madelaine's with Pelon.

There was a burst of cheering across the road.

A large patch had been set up for settling the centuries-old quarrel between the Blackfeet and the Crows, whose firefighter teams had fought shoulder-to-shoulder in the mountains, and who now fought toe-to-toe for the hell of it.

Benny Klein looked on benevolently.

"I'll let 'em kill each other off," he had said earlier.

Farther back some Comanches were trying conclusions with Apaches.

It was a real good Montana party, with fewer than thirty laws being broken in plain view, nothing to worry about.

Bart was sitting in his big SUV, quietly watching the fun. He'd paid for most of it, after all.

Madelaine sighed.

"We got, find him a woman," she said.

Bart's luck with women was a good deal south of atrocious.

A young Indian wearing a yellow fire shirt walked across the road, his eyes on the ground, and when he got to Du Pré and Madelaine he looked up.

"That fire song," he said, "I have heard it, couple places, the coyotes."

"Ah," said Du Pré, "so it is that. I thought so, but them coyotes all know it, eh?"

The young man nodded.

"You are a long way from your people," said Madelaine.

The young man nodded.

"Kiowa," he said. "But I will see them in two days."

"Not good to be away from the people too long," said Madelaine.

He shook his head.

"Thank you," he said. He pulled something from his pocket and he offered it to Madelaine. She held out her hand and he dropped something in her palm, nodded, and walked away.

She waited until he was gone in the crowd before she looked at it.

A canine tooth, a coyote's, pierced for a thong.

Madelaine held up the ivory to Du Pré.

"Nice young man," said Madelaine. "Good manners. It is for you Du Pré."

Madelaine tucked the tooth in the watch pocket of Du Pré's Levi's.

"OK," said Du Pré, "I play it again next time we are playing."

That was what the young man had come to ask, courteously.

The firefighters were drinking huge quantities of beer. Fighting fires is very thirsty work.

There were dozens of half-barrels standing in tubs of ice here and there, and plenty more in the big cooler in the saloon.

"Wonder if we will ever know all of it," said Madelaine.

Du Pré looked at her.

"Nancy Wyman she is in that Warm Springs. Justin is in jail.

Maddy and Billie are dead. Frazier, whoever he is, dead, too. Dykstra is dead, the kids are dead, lots of dead. Why?"

Du Pré shook his head.

Old fires, old scars, old fears, until a last mad blaze.

And that bastard Frazier feeding the flames.

Smart.

I never know why he bother to save me.

Just never know, Du Pré thought.

The rock band boomed and screeched.

"Jesus," said Madelaine, "let's us go inside save our ears."

They went into the cool dark saloon.

There were a few people there, and Susan Klein was on her stool behind the bar. Even now she couldn't stand very long without hurting.

She poured some pink wine for Madelaine and she made a ditch for Du Pré.

Madelaine fished out the coyote tooth from Du Pré's pocket and she went behind the bar and found the little box of beads and buffalo sinew she kept there so she could work when she was tending bar.

She put the tooth on some sinew, enough so Du Pré could slip it over his head.

When he put the coyote-tooth charm on, the bone tapped against the pearl button on his shirt.

"How's it going?" said Susan.

"The music," said Madelaine, "it is pret' good."